BETWEEN RAINS

PACIFIC BAY SERIES - BOOK 4

KELLIE COATES GILBERT

Copyright © 2021 by Kellie Coates Gilbert LLC

Published by Amnos Media Group

All rights reserved.

Cover design: The Killion Group

No part of this book may be reproduced in any form or by any electronic or mechanical means, including information storage and retrieval systems, without written permission from the author, except for the use of brief quotations in a book review.

www.kelliecoatesgilbert.com

This book is dedicated to two dear friends who have stood alongside me on this publishing journey, cheering and waving pom-poms. I love you two.

Joanne Kimey
Nancy Patrick

WHAT OTHERS ARE SAYING ABOUT KELLIE'S BOOKS

"Well-drawn, sympathetic characters and graceful language"
~**Library Journal**

"Deft, crisp storytelling"
~**RT Book Reviews**

"I devoured the book in one sitting."
~**Chick Lit Central**

"Gilbert's heartfelt fiction is always a pleasure to read."
~**Buzzing About Books**

ALSO BY KELLIE COATES GILBERT

THE PACIFIC BAY SERIES

Chances Are

Remember Us

Chasing Wind

Between Rains

THE SUN VALLEY SERIES

Sisters

Heartbeats

Changes

Promises

LOVE ON VACATION SERIES

Otherwise Engaged

All Fore Love

TEXAS GOLD SERIES

A Woman of Fortune

Where Rivers Part

A Reason to Stay

What Matters Most

1

Rhett Duvall leaned against the seat and closed his eyes as the plane descended onto the runway. The cabin of an aircraft felt like home to Rhett, he'd flown in them so often. He could curl up and sleep as easily as dozing on the couch, often quipping that a 747 was his sky-born cradle, rocked by the winds far above the ground.

Unlike most people, Rhett enjoyed living out of a suitcase for his job, traveling around the country. Last year, he'd spent two hundred out of three hundred and sixty-five nights in a hotel room. He wasn't complaining, mind you. He'd worked damned hard to get where he was. No one really knew what it had taken to climb to the highest rungs on the Chicago Private Equity Group ladder. His high six-figure salary had cost him vacations, holidays with family, and a fiancée. Personal time was a limited commodity. He couldn't even own a dog.

Some might claim the sacrifices were not worth it. Not him. Rhett Duvall was a man who loved the thrill of chasing a prospect and closing another deal.

The flight attendant's voice rang out over the intercom, "Welcome to the Portland International Airport." She paused.

"We apologize for the bumpy landing. It's not the captain's fault. It's not the co-pilot's fault. I'm afraid it's the asphalt."

Laughter rang out in the cabin.

"For your safety, we ask that you remain seated until the plane comes to a complete stop at the gate. Look people, at no time in history has a passenger beaten a plane to the gate. So please, don't even try. Also, please be careful opening the overhead bins because, as everyone knows, *shift happens.*"

The pretty blonde flight attendant with the intercom device in her hand locked her gaze and flashed him a brilliant smile.

Rhett smiled back. She was a looker, for certain. And friendly.

He wrapped the cord of his noise-canceling earphones neatly, and packed them away in the zipped case, and placed it inside his Italian leather briefcase. When the overhead speaker finally dinged, granting passengers permission to move freely about the cabin, he raised from his plush first-class seat and stretched his legs. He swung the door open on the overhead stowage bin, retrieved his duffel and moved for the open exit.

"Thank you for flying with us, Mr. Duvall." The blonde granted him another wide smile.

Rhett nodded in her direction, then smiled his appreciation to the captain standing beside her. "Great flight," he said before moving out of the plane and onto the jet bridge. Minutes later he stepped into the terminal, surprised at how happy he felt as he took note of the teal carpet with geometric shapes rumored to represent the intersection of the north and south runways seen by air traffic controllers from the airport's tower at night. That carpet was the first sign he was home.

He hadn't returned in what...three years? The realization created a pang of guilt in his gut. He never meant for his absence to be so lengthy. It's just that life and his work... Well, time sometimes got away from him.

Even so, he was good about calling his folks at least a

couple of times a month, usually on Sunday nights. Rhett patiently talked to his mom, listened to her fill him in on everything going on in Pacific Bay—from the weather to who was getting married to who was having children. His dad kept him apprised of how the oyster farm was doing. He knew when the larvae tanks were emptied and the tiny seed was planted in the beds. He listened as his father debated the value of tumbling before harvest and for how long. He knew that, in the end, his dad would always dismiss the idea that manually stimulating growth would be the chosen route. "Despite what these so-called scientific experts claim, bottom culturing does the trick sufficiently and grows strong shells, son. That's always been my take."

Rhett's stomach growled. Perhaps he shouldn't have skipped the in-flight meal. He pulled his cell phone from his jacket pocket and hit the car rental company number he had on speed dial. When a man answered, Rhett cleared his throat. "Yeah, I know it's late, but I think I'm going to grab a bite before picking up the car. Is that all right?"

"Absolutely, Mr. Duvall. Just call when you're ready, and we'll have your rental waiting out at valet parking."

Rhett thanked him and pocketed his phone, headed through the terminal past security, and made his way to Stanford's, where he ordered grilled salmon with lemon-chive crème sauce, a side salad topped with bay shrimp, and a glass of bourbon.

Outside the rain-drizzled window, distant lights from across the Columbia River broke through the darkness. The precipitation was no surprise. Portland averaged over a hundred days of rain a year. Often, especially in the spring, barely a day would pass between rains.

"The important thing is the life you live in between rains," his mother was often known to say.

"Hey, there." The female voice caught Rhett's attention. He

turned to see the blonde flight attendant smiling back at him. "Mind if I join you?"

He did, but he was too polite to say so. Not that he didn't enjoy time with a beautiful woman, but tonight he was tired and had a lot on his mind. There were rumors the firm was facing some big changes. He'd weathered restructures and buyouts before, but business interruptions were never welcome, especially when the rumor mill ramped up and his clients started calling.

Without waiting for a reply, the woman from the plane slid into the chair opposite him. "You travel much?" she asked, waving over the waitress.

"Yeah. Some say too much," he replied, abandoning his quiet evening to himself.

"I'm Heather." She held out her hand.

He shook. "Rhett." He knew from experience that airport romances were often short-lived and on a one-name basis.

She glanced at his ringless-finger. "You married?"

He shook his head, chuckled. "To my work, I suppose." He didn't bother telling her he'd been engaged once and that it hadn't worked out, or that his second long-term relationship had gone south as well.

Her face broke into a smile. "Yeah, I totally get where you're coming from. I was married. Twice. This flying gig is hard on relationships."

He suspected from her bold approach that additional factors might have played into her past marital discord. A guess on his part, but he'd seen the type often. In fact, something inside told him he might not have to sleep alone tonight, if he so elected. It was a feeling, not something he'd necessarily act on. He'd grown tired of the hit-and-run relationships a while ago. Besides, he planned to get on the road and drive straight through to Pacific Bay after he finished his dinner.

A waitress appeared at their table and handed Heather a menu.

"Kids?" she asked as she looked it over. She turned to the waitress, "A crab salad please. Dressing on the side." She glanced at his glass of bourbon. "And what he's having."

Again, he shook his head. "Nope. Never had the time for children." He briefly explained his career and the demands it made on his life.

She straightened the fork on the table. "So, is that what brings you to Portland? Business?"

"Not this time. I'm in Oregon to see family. They live in a tiny tourist town on the coast called Pacific Bay. My dad and mom own an oyster farm, one that has been in our family for three generations."

"An oyster farm? How interesting. You know what they say about oysters?" She grinned suggestively.

"Yeah, don't believe everything you read." He lifted his glass and drained the remaining alcohol before motioning to the bartender that he'd like another.

A young woman entered the restaurant, juggling an unwieldy stroller, one of those double-kind, while trying to keep hold of an active little toddler. She looked near tears with the stress of it all. He immediately felt for her. It couldn't be easy.

The waitress delivered Heather's salad.

"My family lives in Florida," she explained, picking up her fork. "Well, my mom and dad. I have no siblings. My parents are retired." She drizzled dressing across the plate of chopped lettuce piled with fresh crab meat. "Goodness, this looks delicious. I've been flying Midwest routes. I'm afraid you can't get good seafood in Kansas." She sighed.

He nodded. Yes, seafood was plentiful in the Pacific Northwest...and delicious. He planned on taking advantage of the fact during his short visit.

"So, tell me more about your family," she prodded.

Rhett shrugged. "Not too much to tell, really. My sister, Leila...well, she's married and has three kids."

"Yeah? What does her husband do?"

"Not much," he admitted, letting a chuckle escape his lips. "He's a full-time dreamer. One of those who is always going to hit it big with the next thing. He's like a moth drawn to light when it comes to those pyramid selling schemes. First, it was essential oils. Then he talked my sister into becoming an online make-up consultant. They've sold vitamins, toys, household cleaning products. Wes, that's my brother-in-law's name, well... he's the king of eBay and Etsy accounts, and he swears he makes hundreds a month with his Amazon affiliate account. Funny thing, though...he's always borrowing from my folks to make rent."

Heather wrinkled her nose. "Oh, yikes."

"Yeah." The waitress delivered his second glass of bourbon. He took it and smiled at her with appreciation. "My brother works with my folks on the oyster farm. He's a bit of a...well, let's just say we're not exactly close. He has a little trouble embracing the concept of growing up."

"Not like you," she remarked. "I mean, your position and what you've done in life is impressive."

"Thanks. I like to think that, despite my humble roots, I made something of myself." He heard pride swell absurdly in his voice and tried to push it away.

Out of the corner of his eye, he saw the young mother lift two infants from the stroller, expertly nesting one in each arm. This allowed the young toddler to escape her clutch. The little boy ran wildly around the table while his mother attempted in vain to hush him.

Was she...crying?

Rhett wiped the corner of his mouth with the linen napkin,

never taking his eyes off the struggling mother. "Uh, Heather. Could you excuse me for a moment?"

His tablemate looked confused as he lifted from his seat at the table. Not bothering to fold his napkin, Rhett tossed it down next to his plate and made his way across the restaurant to the young woman. "You look like you could use some help." He dropped down and motioned for the little guy to come closer. "Hey, are you a superhero? Because I really like superheroes."

The little brown-haired toddler stopped cold. "Yup. And I can fly." To prove his point, he held out both arms in front of his body Superman-style and ran in a circle.

Rhett grinned and looked up at his mother. "Well, I know from experience that superheroes need to eat in order to keep up their superpowers. You up for a cheeseburger, kiddo?"

He assisted the appreciative mother and got the kid settled in his seat. When finished, he leaned over and glanced at her babies in her arms. "Sweet kids."

"Thank you so much," she said. "I—well, my flight was delayed, and my car rental office is closed. We were hungry, so I thought we'd catch a bite before I called a cab. It's a lot." She gave him a weak smile. "But I got it now. Thank you."

Rhett pulled his phone and quickly texted. "Look, I have a car waiting. You're welcome to it." He told her where the car would be parked.

"Oh, I can't do that," she insisted.

"Sure, you can. I'll call a cab and head to a hotel, then grab another car in the morning. All's good," he assured her. As an added measure, he waved over the waitress. "Please add her dinner to my tab." He turned back to the young mother. "Take care of those little ones."

"I will," she said, grateful tears glistening. "I—I don't know how to thank you."

Rhett drew a deep breath, pleased that he'd come to her

rescue. The effort was small but obviously meant a lot to her. He turned and headed back in the direction of his table, now empty.

He glanced around and located the flight attendant at the bar talking with a guy in a suit. Rhett threw some bills on the table, enough to cover both his meal and his departed dinner mate's salad, plus that of the young mother with the kiddos. The polite thing might be to walk over and bid Heather goodnight before he left. But she looked far too interested in her new prospect, and he didn't want to interrupt.

A slight smile pulled at the corner of his lips as he saw her place a manicured hand on the sleeve of the guy's arm and laugh. She caught him watching. Rhett gave her a gracious nod before downing his drink. Then he shrugged and headed for the door.

2

It was a strange kind of autumn morning in Pacific Bay. Two days earlier, a north wind blew in from Alaska, bringing unseasonal frigid temps and, with it, a heavy marine layer off the coast. Despite the thick fog, Rhett could make out familiar landmarks as he passed the iconic welcome sign at the edge of town.

Pacific Bay was one of those unique communities along the rugged Oregon coastline that beckoned tourists and still provided a small-town feel for those who called the place home. Main Street ran along the edge of the bay filled with fishing boats. Seafood canneries bordered the water's edge. Gift shops selling souvenirs and T-shirts and restaurants offering steaming bowls of clam chowder and platters of crab legs lined the area.

Homes with stunning views of the coastline dotted the cliffs overlooking the Pacific Ocean. Long beaches stretched for miles, providing joggers and dogwalkers the perfect wide-open stretches of sand with frothy waves creeping onshore. A lighthouse nearly one-hundred-feet tall perched at the westernmost point of the basalt headland surrounded by tidal pools teeming with starfish and bright-colored anemones.

Despite the visually diminished conditions, Rhett saw each of these familiar elements clearly in his mind's eye as he drove through town.

He searched for the power button that would lower the car window so he could breathe deeply, take in the salty air. It had been far too long since he'd experienced the way the atmosphere carried a pungent smell of fish mixed with pine from the surrounding trees. He loved the aroma—the smell of home.

Up ahead, about a mile, was the turnoff to the eight-mile winding road that circled the outer bay, the route that led to his destination...a brackish backwater inlet lined with tall Douglas firs and native woodland ferns, some the size of a German Shepherd.

Home was the Pacific Bay Oyster Farm, which was something of a Pacific Bay institution. The original owners had opened the flourishing business back at the turn of the century, selling to Rhett's ancestors in the forties. The oyster operation had been passed down from generation to generation and currently was in the capable hands of his father, Wylie Duvall.

Together, his parents had taken the oyster-growing business to another level, adding a retail shop and international shipping. They also sponsored and held an annual oyster feed attended by hundreds of locals and tourists from several surrounding states. The popular event was once featured in *Sunset Magazine*, which had his mom flustered because she thought her years were starting to show. "I don't want my picture taken for all those people to see," she argued.

His sister, Leila, quickly assured her the images could be photoshopped. "That's what all the Hollywood celebrities do, Mom. Don't worry. Those people can erase every wrinkle."

His dad had sidled up behind his wife. "Oh, Grace. You

know you're the most beautiful woman in the world in my eyes. What does it matter what others think?"

His mom flushed with embarrassment and playfully pushed him aside. "Good to hear. But we all know that you are half-blind."

Rhett braked, slowing for the final bend in the road. Despite the lack of cars crowding the roadway, out of habit, he turned on his blinker before exiting onto the long drive made of tiny white oyster shell fragments. He pulled up to the front door of the retail shop and cut the engine.

Even at this early hour, he could see activity out on the wooden pier, knew that workers were preparing for the day. The store wouldn't open until ten, but hours of work would be behind them before his mom tied her apron around her waist and turned the sign hanging on the glass front door to *Open*.

Rhett exited the car, dragging his duffel with him. He knew his mom would be peering out the kitchen window of her house located to the east of the store and across a wide span of green lawn bordered with beds filled with colorful mums and dahlias. His mom was proud of her flowers and had carefully cultivated her planting so that every season put on a show.

He didn't even make it to the sidewalk before the front door opened and she scrambled out, wiping her hands on a towel. "There you are!"

His mom pulled him into a tight hug, kissed him on the cheek. "Oh, look what I've done," she said, wiping at the smear of her signature red lipstick her smooch had left behind.

There was a hint of moisture in her eyes, which created a pang of guilt deep inside Rhett's gut. He shouldn't have let so much time pass.

"Come," she beckoned, taking hold of his arm and pulling him toward the front door.

Inside, the large living room was empty, except for some carefully placed leather sofas and a few occasional tables. Past the large windows overlooking the water stood the connected kitchen where excited shouts of children filled the air as two young boys charged for their uncle, taking his legs into their chubby arms in a death grip. The littlest one quickly pulled his head back. "Did you bring us something? Mommy said you would."

Rhett laughed and bent down, pulled two five-dollar bills from his back pocket, tucked there earlier for this very occasion. "Here you go. I hear you guys are now old enough to handle a little cash."

The oldest's eyes grew wide. He reached for his money. "Thanks, Uncle Rhett."

"I'm four now," reported the youngest, holding up as many fingers before claiming his money.

Rhett ruffled the tops of both their heads before straightening. His sister stood at the stove, frying bacon. She turned and smiled back at him as he approached. "Hey, there. Nice to have you home."

He scooped her into a hug.

"Careful!" she warned. "I don't want you to get burned."

He responded by slipping a piece of crisp bacon from the plate on the counter and popping it into his mouth.

She slapped at his hand. "Hey!" She pointed to the table set with plates and silverware. "Sit. Breakfast is nearly ready."

Rhett did as he was instructed, taking the seat he'd occupied as a teen, out of habit. "Where's Dad and Jared?" he asked, scanning the familiar room—the pine cupboards, the countertops filled with clutter and the side-by-side refrigerator, a Christmas gift to his mother despite the fact she argued her old one still worked just fine.

His mom peered out the window above the sink. "Jared ran an errand to Astoria. Left at the crack of dawn. I don't know what could be holding your father up. He knew you were coming."

Rhett shrugged and gave his mother a smile. "I'm sure he'll be in soon."

They both knew Wylie Duvall believed in hard work. Few beat him up in the morning and it was a rare man who outlasted him out in the mudflats. How many times had Rhett heard his dad say, "Oysters don't wait, son."

While no one specifically asked, Leila reported her husband would be joining them soon as well. "Wes was up late learning to start a YouTube channel," she explained. "I told him to sleep in."

Their mom pointed in the direction of the window in the living room. "Looks like Wes is here now."

Little Levi, the four-year-old, piped up, "Yeah, Daddy doesn't like to miss breakfast. He can eat more pancakes than anybody."

His brother nodded enthusiastically. "Yeah, once he eated fifteen!"

Leila gave her son a look. "Don't exaggerate." She turned to Rhett. "The most he's eaten in one sitting is a dozen, and that was down at the Pig 'n' Pancake when the boys from town all challenged him."

The door burst open, and in walked Wes.

Rhett scowled in confusion as he lifted from the table. Had his brother-in-law grown shorter since he'd last seen him? No, must be he'd gained weight, providing for a more rotund figure and the illusion of a loss of height. Frankly, that was the least of his flaws.

"Rhett!" Wes grabbed his hand and shook with fervor, nearly wrenching Rhett's arm from its socket. "Long time, no see, buddy."

"Hey," Rhett replied, wanting to rub his wounded shoulder.

Wes clapped his hands and headed for the table. "What's there to eat? I'm starving!"

Leila smiled and carried a platter of crisp bacon to the table and set it before her husband, who quickly scooped about a third of the strips onto his plate before tucking his napkin at the chin of his plaid flannel shirt. "So, sit," he told Rhett. "Tell us all about that fancy Chicago town. I hear they have the best pizza. And hot dogs. That right?"

Rhett sank back down into his spot at the table. "Some think so." He looked over at his mother. "Are we going to wait for Dad?"

A brief look of concern crossed her face. "Leila, sweetie. Would you go down to the sheds and see what's keeping him?"

Leila nodded. "Sure, Mama."

"There's Papa!" Little Levi pointed out the glass window. "He's coming."

Sure enough, Rhett's dad was lumbering up the from the barns, crossing the lawn with a hose coiled over his shoulder. Rhett stood for a second time and waited for the door to open.

A minute or so passed. His mom pulled the apron from her waist and tossed it on the counter. "I'll go get him."

Minutes later, she re-entered the kitchen, followed by his dad. "Hey, Pop," Rhett said in greeting. He moved for his old man and pulled him into an embrace, then leaned back, looked his dad over. "Good to see you, old man."

A confused look formed on his father's face. "Rhett? What are you doing here, son?" He turned to his wife. "Why didn't you tell me Rhett was coming?"

Grace and Leila exchanged glances before Rhett's mom patted her husband's back. "Honey, I did. I told you Rhett's plane landed last night and that he'd be here this morning."

Little Levi repositioned himself on his seat so he was leaning forward on his knees. He reached across the table for a strip of bacon. "Papa forgets stuff sometimes," he said, mimicking his father by shoving the entire crispy strip in his mouth.

Rhett's sister quickly moved to the boy's side, diverted his attention. "Careful, you'll choke," she warned. "Now sit down on that chair right and wait for the rest of us."

"But, Mommy..."

"Sit," she repeated.

Rhett's eyes narrowed. He gazed back at his mother, searched her face.

She quickly averted her attention away from his scrutiny and grabbed her apron, tied it back in place around her waist. "Now, who wants pancakes?"

3

Rhett hadn't seen his brother in person in over...what? Four years? Jared had been on a backpacking trip with friends the last time Rhett was in Oregon. During the span of his absence, they'd rarely spoken, instead exchanging texts or voicemails every few months, occasionally catching each other running out the door to work or social engagements.

"Sorry, Dude. Heading out."

"No worries. TTYL."

Rhett had his assistant send a card on his birthday every year, even though Jared failed to reciprocate. Rhett kept up on his brother mainly through his parents but often wondered if their reports were entirely accurate. Both remained strong champions of every one of their offspring, despite any hiccups in character...especially in Jared's case.

Jared lived alone on a decommissioned fishing trawler anchored at the shoreline only yards away from the sheds. Rhett knew he'd likely have pulled himself from his unmade bed, pulled on his waders and was already down at the shucking shed by dawn...even after a long night of partying with his buddies down at the Sea Star Tavern. His brother lacked a lot of personal qualities, but work ethic was not one of them.

Rhett carried a steaming mug of coffee and made his way in that direction, remembering his mother's words from the prior evening. "He's a different person now," she said, putting an arm around Rhett's shoulder as they walked the hall to their respective bedrooms late last night.

At first, Rhett didn't recognize his brother. He was twenty-six now, his hair a bit shorter, skin tan and taut over his relaxed facial features. The last time Rhett had seen him he'd still seemed a boy, really—round face marked with acne, hair in wild curls cascading to the edge of his shirt collar, a childish slouch to his bony shoulders. Apparently, he hadn't stopped growing and now topped Rhett by a couple of inches, maybe more.

Upon approach, Jared put out his hand. "Hey, bro."

Rhett grabbed it firmly, tugged him forward to his chest, slapped both hands against his back. He pulled from his brother's embrace, leaned back, and looked briefly into Jared's eyes, which were filtered by a pair of scratched aviators perched on his nose. "Good to see you," he told him, with as much genuine feeling as he could muster.

"Yeah, you too." With one finger, Jared reached inside the lens of his glasses and rubbed at his eye. "Been a while."

Yet another pang of guilt unfurled in Rhett's gut. It had been too long. He didn't need to be reminded.

Jared locked his hands behind his head, fingers lost in the tangled mass of brown hair. "You staying long?"

"Nah, just here for Dad's big birthday celebration."

Jared nodded. "Yeah, seventy-five years. A milestone." He paused. "Uh, sorry I didn't make it last night. Got hung up in Astoria. Long story."

Rhett knew better than to ask for details. Jared's stories

often fostered judgment on his part, and he'd promised himself to just chill on this trip. Wasn't worth another battle over things he couldn't change. And if he'd learned anything, he'd learned his brother would never change.

Despite the possibility of a wrestling scholarship, Jared had dropped out of high school only weeks from graduation. When their mother had called to report this to Rhett, he'd immediately gone into *fix it* mode. He'd immediately made a quick trip home and chewed the snot-nosed little flake out. "Geez, Jared. Are you kidding me? What do you think you're doing? Do you know the hell you're putting Mom through? And Dad?"

"Stay out of it," Jared warned.

"Look, if you need help studying, maybe I could—" Rhett began, but Jared cut him off, kicking himself away from the table, the chair rocking backward, nearly toppling.

"Butt out!" he'd demanded before storming from the room.

Rhett fumed for weeks after, telling anyone who would listen, even some of his coworkers back in Chicago, "Jared's a loser. He never thinks of anybody but himself." Initially, they all thought him harsh; he could tell. But that was because they didn't know the number of times his younger brother had been arrested for driving while under the influence. They didn't know about the girls he slept with, girls that were already in relationships with his friends. They sure didn't know how, despite all this, his parents deemed his little brother the favorite—always defending him. They started throwing around words like "depression," "therapy," and "medication," as if the answer to their son's behavior could all be found on the internet.

And Jared's finances? Rhett couldn't help but shake his head. His younger brother made his brother-in-law look good —like a friggin' Bill Gates, in comparison.

The truth was, Jared was too immature and lazy to apply himself. A good time trumped responsibility at every turn.

What really topped the cake was when his mother called to report she'd received a heartfelt letter a few months ago, penned by a repentant son...a plea for forgiveness and promising to turn his behavior around. While on the phone with Rhett, his mother wept. "And he has, Rhett. You should see him. He's hardly the same boy we raised. I'd go through the whole thing again just to get that letter."

Rhett remained doubtful. In his experience, people didn't often change overnight. In fact, they often never did.

Jared slipped off the sleeves of his flannel shirt, revealing a fading tattoo, what looked to be barbed wire ringing his bicep. "Well, I'd better get to it. We've got a shipment of spat we have to broadcast this morning before they start to spawn in the containers."

Rhett nodded. "Need some help?"

Jared pulled a hand through the top of his hair before shaking his head. "No, got it handled. See you up at the house for lunch?" Before Rhett could respond, he quietly added, "Hey, bro. I'm glad you're home."

Rhett felt his whole face alter, his mouth lose its rigid set. "Sure, yeah. See you up there."

He turned and walked slowly toward the house, the heels of his boots hitting the weathered wood on the dock in rhythm while taking in long breaths of the mist-filled air.

An odd truth suddenly resonated.

This place—these people, were his anchor.

4

Steps from the back door, Rhett bent to pick some wild daisies that had sprouted along the porch like weeds, tucked the bunch behind his back, and opened the door. His mom turned from the sink where she was washing dishes.

Rhett ceremoniously pulled the bouquet from behind his back, just like he did back when he was ten. "There's the prettiest girl in all of Pacific Bay, right there." He kissed his mom's cheek, delighting in the smile that immediately formed on her face.

"Oh, well...there my boy goes again. Sweeping all the pretty ones off their feet."

Rhett turned toward the voice to see his dad approaching, his hair still wet from the shower. He smiled and moved to embrace his dad, enjoying the feel of his father's arms tucked tightly around his shoulders. "Morning, Pop. Sleep well?"

His dad laughed. "Sleep's overrated. Been up for hours. Where you been?"

Rhett nodded in the direction of the water's edge. "Down at the sheds."

"You want some coffee, Wylie?" Without waiting for a reply, Rhett's mom reached for the cupboard. She pulled out a mug and moved for the coffee pot on the counter.

"Did you see your brother?" his dad asked.

"Yeah. Jared was down there."

His mom handed her husband the steaming mug, then turned to Rhett. "You want some too, honey?"

"Sure. But I can get it."

She waved him off. "No, let me." She filled another mug and motioned for him to sit at the table, then placed the mug in front of him.

His dad leaned with his back against the counter and took a sip. "That boy has really stepped up lately," his dad reported. "He's been working hard. Learning the business. Been a big help around here."

"That's right," his mom chimed in. "Your brother's been a lifesaver. He does the work of three laborers. And he's even helping me with some of the retail end of things over at the store."

"Yup, seems that boy has finally turned the corner." His dad stared into his mug, swallowed visibly. "There were times I wondered if Jared would ever get his life together. But the past is the past. The best thing about waking up each morning is the fact you face a new day."

"Only took years on my knees," his mom reminded. She pointed to her legs. "You should see the callouses that formed on my knees from all those prayers." She gave them a wide grin with her bright-red lipstick in place.

Rhett laughed, a bit tinnily. "Well, I hope you're right," he said, cautiously. Did he need to remind them of the earlier occasions when they thought Jared had experienced a change of character only to discover their youngest son had found yet another way to break their hearts?

"Drink up, boy. I want to show you the renovations we've

made." His dad lifted his mug and downed his remaining coffee.

Grace wiped her hands on her apron. "You were absolutely right to urge us to invest in some improvements, Rhett." She turned to her husband. "Our boy knows his finances."

"Well, he darn-tootin' should," he said. "I'd like to think that leaving the operation and his family behind meant something in the end."

Ouch. Rhett cleared his throat and placed his coffee cup in the sink with a little too much force. Perhaps his father was teasing. He loved to joke around. Often though, his ribbing was a hidden front for a more serious jab. Despite the fact his dad would not come right out and voice his displeasure with Rhett's choices, there was no mistaking that, by moving away, he'd disappointed him on some level.

Of course, none of his family really understood his aspirations were much higher than digging in the mud and spending free hours down at the Sea Star drinking with the guys he'd grown up with. Jared had those bases covered.

Truth was, his family barely knew him. They knew the version that grew up in Pacific Bay, the star half-back on the high school football team, the guy who actually liked to study and graduated at the top of his class—the son, brother, and friend to everyone. But they didn't know *him*.

He'd gone to school only an hour or so away from Pacific Bay. Yet none of his family ever visited while he was at the University of Oregon, never set foot in any of his dorm rooms. His mom and dad did attend the graduation ceremony, but had to rush back. His dad was in the middle of filling his first international shipment, and they were on a deadline to pull and shuck before the shipping containers were loaded in Astoria, taking the harvest to those swanky hotel buffets in Hong Kong. "Oysters don't wait on anybody, son."

He wasn't complaining exactly. He loved his family. But he'd never quite understood why planes only flew one direction. He'd half hoped to convince his parents to make a trip to Chicago, let him show them the sights...the Art Institute where original Picasso and Chagall paintings hung in all their glory, maybe catch a live performance at Lurie Garden, or maybe take them to the top of Willis Tower. On a clear day, you could stand on the Skydeck and see forty to fifty miles over four states, gaining a bird's eye view of the Windy City.

Realistically, he knew his folks weren't the sort to embrace the cultural side of his beloved city, but he could have at least taken his dad to Wrigley Field. How many times had his mom mentioned, "Isn't that where Oprah Winfrey lives?" Each time he'd carefully explain that her favorite celebrity's production company was headquartered in the heart of Chicago, but she had multiple homes. "I doubt Oprah lives here much of the time."

His mother had agreed with him over the phone. "True. I heard she had a big home in Maui." She paused. "Now, that's the way to live."

"You want to go to Hawaii, Mom? I can take you."

She waved him off. "Oh, that's far too expensive. Besides, your dad would never leave our operation that long, and I would never go and leave him behind."

And that's the way it went.

He tried not to be resentful or allow the notion much room in his head. The truth was, he was part of their lives. They were not necessarily part of his. The worst part was they didn't even see it. If they did, the disparity didn't seem to matter.

"Ready?" his dad asked, placing his empty mug in the sink.

Rhett nodded and lifted from the table, his own mug in hand. He started to clear the remnants of breakfast.

"Leave it, honey. I'll clean up," his mom told him. "You go with your father. He has a lot he wants to show you."

Rhett spent the rest of the day out in the sheds with his dad.

While much was the same, much had changed in the time he'd been away. His dad was notorious for being a spendthrift. He believed if you didn't have the funds in hand, you didn't spend. It had been an effort for Rhett to convince his parents that leveraging the assets could increase cash flow and free up money to invest, manifesting even more long-term value.

While his parents hadn't taken his advice in its entirety, they had taken out a small business loan which had allowed them to replace the worn, antiquated hi-flow system, purchase new downweller tanks, and double their tumblers, sorters, and washers. The expenditure was quickly paid back with the increased production. New employees had been added to the payroll, and his dad was able to focus more attention on international trade efforts. All in all, his recommendations had paid off.

The retail store, however, still needed attention...at least, as far as he could see. The interior looked the same as it had in the early sixties. He'd seen photographs to prove it.

A large wooden sign posted at the entrance read "Pacific Bay Oysters – Founded 1907."

The store itself was rather nondescript—a wooden building painted white with no architectural features to speak of. At either side of the entrance, metal benches painted green lined the doorway. A large pot of pink petunias with flowing blue lobelia was the only indication the building was a retail outlet and not another processing structure.

Inside, linoleum stretched across the small space to a glass-cased counter that held a variety of Cryovac bags filled with smoked oysters. In addition to the regular variety, some were hickory-smoked, some barbeque flavored, and some were flavored with garlic. Floor-to-ceiling metal coolers with glass doors lined the wall. Inside were large netted bags filled with oysters in the shell...Pacific, Hama Hamas, and Kumomotos, which were small but delicious. Nutty and sweet.

They also grew and sold Olympias, the only oyster strictly native to Pacific waters. Again, small in size but big in rich, mineral flavor. Olympias tended to be a little persnickety to grow, which meant few producers bothered. The upside is that they brought a premium price on the market.

Out back, there was a fryer. His mom would make batter daily and fry up a batch of oysters made-to-order. Customers often took advantage of the wooden picnic tables and the view, which was magnificent this time of the year. Autumn foliage at the coast never disappointed, with all the fiery reds and oranges of maturing native grapevines and golden leaves of walnut trees and cottonwoods tucked in among towering pines.

After touring the facilities, Rhett and his dad sat at one of the picnic tables while carrying tall Styrofoam cups of iced tea. "So, Jared. What did you think of all the improvements?"

"Rhett."

His father looked at him, puzzled. "What?"

"You called me Jared." Rhett swirled the brown liquid in his Styrofoam cup and took a swig.

"Oh. Sorry. Honest mistake." His dad took off his cap and set it down on the table. "So, what did you think, son?"

"I like it," Rhett assured him. "You've done a lot of work here, Pop. It shows. And from what you and Mom are telling me, and backed by the numbers I'm seeing, it's paying off."

His dad's gaze wandered down to the water's edge. "We still have a lot to do." He took out a tiny wire-bound notebook from his shirt pocket and a pen. He drew out his ideas for expanding. "By adding maturation tanks, we should be able to reduce predatory losses of our spat."

Rhett nodded in agreement. "And with the operation loan in place, you'll likely be able to take that addition on next spring. We might even be able to negotiate a reduction in interest rate when we provide the year-end income and loss statements."

"Well, speak of the devil," his dad said, nodding in the direction of the pier. "There's your brother now."

Rhett followed his gaze to see Jared approaching. In the distance, his brother tugged a draped T-shirt from his bare shoulders and pulled it over his head, taking care not to knock the Aviator sunglasses perched at the top of his hair.

Rhett let out a brief, uneasy chuckle. "So, who's the kid dating these days?"

"No one in particular. The boy's grown up, quit the drinking...the partying."

Rhett listened to his father praise his brother for only a short while before he diverted the subject. "Well, if he's become such a big help, sounds like maybe you and Mom could pull away for a little trip. Maybe come to Chicago for a visit?" he prodded hopefully.

Before his dad could respond, Jared sauntered up. "Hey," he said.

"Hey," Rhett replied back.

His brother shuffled on his feet. "I was thinking—well, when you're through here, maybe we could go into town for a drink?"

Rhett scowled. "I thought you gave up—"

Jared laughed. "I'm strictly Coca-Cola these days. But that doesn't mean we can't stop off at the Sea Star. Thought you might like to connect with some of the boys."

Their father's eyes brightened at the suggestion. "That's a fine idea. You boys go out, and I'll grab that pretty mother of yours and scoop her out to dinner as well. A date."

Jared grinned. "Good luck with talking her into that."

"I'll tell her we'll walk the beach after. How can she refuse?"

Jared remained skeptical but seemed to let it go. "Sounds like a plan." He turned his attention to Rhett. "So, you in? It'll give us a chance to catch up."

What was there to catch up on that his mother hadn't

already told him over the phone? He knew that Jared had spent time in rehab last year, that he'd enrolled in some online college courses offered by Oregon State—an accounting course and a marine biology course. Come spring, he intended to add what would amount to full-time credits while still working full-time at the oyster farm. According to his mother and dad, Jared had been diligently saving his wages and planned to build a small house down the road from the farm on a little plot of land that had recently gone up for sale.

Maybe this goodwill gesture had been extended out of some secret need. That was it! Jared was going to ask something of him beyond what he was willing to give. He didn't want to get involved in his brother's finances or give advice. He certainly didn't want to be asked to co-sign a loan. Of course, his parents would likely step up to that plate. They'd always been his private benefactor and bailed him out of financial trouble in the past. It wasn't unlikely they'd try and help him now if he fell short of needed funds. Frankly, he wasn't sure how his parents ever stayed ahead, what with lending to his no-good brother-in-law and saving Jared at every turn.

Even so, Rhett couldn't seem to come up with a viable excuse to turn down his brother's offer. "Sure, okay. I guess I could go for a quick beer."

5

Rhett and Jared arrived at the Sea Star just before happy hour. The parking lot was filled with an array of vehicles, many belonging to guys coming in off the fishing vessels and wanting to enjoy a beer before they headed home to their families.

"This place never changes," Rhett noted as he followed Jared to the entrance.

"Yeah, guess you're right," he replied. "Part of me appreciates the fact that, in a world often tilting with every wave, some things remain the same. Kind of provides an anchor."

Rhett couldn't help but frown. When had his little brother turned philosophical?

When Rhett stepped inside, it took several seconds for his eyes to adjust to the dim light. The first thing he saw was the familiar pendant on the wall behind the bar—the one he and his teammates had all signed after winning the state championship. One of those players, his best friend from high school, now sat around a table at the back, near the old-fashioned jukebox with neon lighting. A Lynyrd Skynyrd song played.

"There he is!" Ben stood and waved them over.

Cam Davis was also at the table. Despite his being older, Rhett had easily bonded with Cam. He was one of the good ones, and Rhett was grateful to call him a close friend.

Rhett waved back and headed that way, wandering past the bar where a few haggard-looking men sat on stools, nursing their drinks. One was smoking. In the back, a couple of fishermen he recognized from down on the wharf were playing pool.

He made his way to the small, varnished wooden table where his buddies sat. Ben rubbed at his chiseled chin, rough with growth, before pulling Rhett into a brief embrace. "Good to see you, bud," he said, with a pat on the back.

Cam stood and extended his hand. "Been a while," he said, shaking Rhett's hand. "You're looking good. The city must agree with you."

Rhett took a seat. "Yeah, Chi-Town's been good to me in a lot of ways."

Jared nodded in the direction of the bathroom. "I'll be right back," he promised.

"What can I get you?" the bartender asked, a towel tucked at his waistline.

Rhett pulled the menu. He was in the mood for a craft beer, maybe a dark stout or porter. Without looking, he knew the choices would be slim. Even so, he was surprised to find they'd added a few selections. "I'll try one of those Rogue River Lagers," he said. "And my brother—" he paused, glanced around, unsure what to order.

Cam grinned at the bartender. "Bring Jared his usual, Axel."

His usual? "So, you guys all still hang out here often," he prompted. "With Jared?"

Both Cam and Ben nodded. "Yeah. We see him here. Who do you think keeps us up on what's going on with you?" Cam asked. "It's not like you check in on a weekly basis or anything."

"Yeah," Ben agreed. "And we're not likely to hang out on Facebook, so…"

Rhett smirked. "You jerk. You know I'm not on Facebook." He was on LinkedIn, but why belabor the point? Not likely these guys would understand the importance of developing a professional presence on the social media platform.

A woman's laughter rang out. Rhett looked in that direction to see Carissa Reynolds chalking up a pool cue. She wore a low-cut top and jeans. Her long blonde hair fell carelessly across one shoulder. Across the smoky interior, their gaze met. She waved. "Hey, handsome. Welcome home," she hollered.

Rhett gave her a quick nod. A pleased grin lifted the corner of her lips before she bent across the table and took aim.

"Careful of that one," Ben warned, his voice low.

Jared appeared and took a seat. The bartender slipped in beside him, expertly carrying bottles of Coors Light and a Dr Pepper with a wedge of lemon inserted into the neck of the bottle. In his other hand, he set a frosted mug filled with amber-colored liquid before Rhett.

"This rounds on me," Ben told him, passing the bottles around the table.

Rhett lifted his mug. "So, how's that new baby?" He took a drink and wiped foam from his mouth with his fingers.

Ben chuckled. "Well, girls are definitely different than boys. Timmy slept through the night within weeks. Even after all these months, Rory still wakes up and screams at the top of her lungs."

Rhett smiled inside. It was good seeing his friend happy again after suffering the heartbreaking loss of his son. The tragedy had taken a toll on his marriage. Rhett was saddened to learn from his mother that Ben and Olivia had run into marital trouble and had separated. Thankfully, they'd worked through their anger and hostility and reconciled. Now, they were happy parents of a little girl who had made her grand appearance at the wedding Cam and Allie's wedding ceremony.

He turned to Cam. "And how's married life treating you?"

Cam's eyes twinkled. "I have to admit, it's pretty darn good." Ben and Cam lifted their beer bottles and clinked them together in a toast to wedded bliss.

Rhett and Jared exchanged glances. "We don't have a similar frame of reference, so we'll just take your word for it," Jared remarked. His hand went to Rhett's shoulder. "Listen up, bro. Play your cards right, and you could be next."

Rhett shook his head. "Nah, first I'd have to find someone willing to put up with me. Besides, I'm far too busy for that kind of thing right now."

As if on cue, his phone buzzed in his pocket. He leaned and pulled it out, glanced at the face. "Hey, I gotta call the office."

He excused himself and headed outside, hit call back, and put the phone to his ear. "Hey, Judith. What's up?"

"Rhett, I need you back here. The Markowitz deal is teetering. I need you to shepherd this one to the finish line."

Rhett drew a deep breath and listened as she explained the details. Apparently, the equity partners were starting to get cold feet. "There's a lot of pressure to keep the company profitable landing on Phil Stengel right now," she told him. "He could use you by his side, hold his hand a bit until this thing gets put to bed. It's what you're good at. When can you fly out? Tonight?"

"Judith, I know Stengel is a basket right now. But I assure you the deal is secure. There's nothing I can't take care of from here. I'll set up a Zoom, work my magic with a face-to-face, if necessary. And I'll move my flight up, but not until the day after tomorrow." He didn't expect her to understand how his name would be *mud* if he bailed on the surprise birthday party his mother was throwing for his father's seventy-fifth birthday. He knew his mom. She'd never forgive him.

"Look, Judith. I got this. Promise."

He suffered a long pause before Judith finally replied. "Okay. I'll go with that. But you know the hit we'll take if this one goes south."

Yes, he knew. Every deal was paramount in Judith Sandidge's mind. She said the same remark at every hiccup. And every deal had hiccups. If necessary, he'd have to remind her of that.

Take, for example, the Andover-Michaels merger. Hints of a product liability suit nearly toppled the deal. Rhett saved the day by hiring a public relations firm out of New York known for high-powered influence in all the right circles. Not only did they launch a very effective media blitz countering the allegations, but they arranged for several congressmen, one of which was also a former National Security Advisor, to publicly hint that a military contract might be in the works. That's all it took to turn the situation around.

"Don't worry," he reassured his boss. "I've got this."

He hung up and turned to see Jared leaving. "Hey, where you going?"

"Mom called, and she needs some help with party preparations. Something about a tent arriving a day early and tipping Pop off. He knows about the party."

"Oh, no. Mom's surprise is wrecked?"

Jared nodded. "Yeah, and the tent is the wrong size. She sounded at her wit's end. Look, you stay and catch up. Cam said he'd drive you home."

"Yeah, okay. That'll work." For a moment, Rhett felt bad about not spending the time with his brother, but quickly reminded himself there would be plenty of time. He wasn't leaving for a couple of days.

Back inside, Cam and Ben were in the middle of a discussion about raising children, another subject foreign to him.

"We got Ryan a new iPad, but were careful to place parental

controls. You can't be too careful these days," Cam said before looking up. "Hey, Rhett. Welcome back. Did somebody back at that company forget you're on vacation?"

"Sorry, guys. Work...well, a deal's going a bit south, and they needed my help," he explained.

Ben slowly nodded. "I don't know how you do it. All that high-pressure stuff pounding down on you all the time."

Rhett attempted to describe how rewarding he found his career, how much he loved living in Chicago. Some might not consider the manner in which he spent his time a good thing—take his mother, for example—but she didn't understand the absolute rush he got from closing a deal. Anything he's had to sacrifice was worth the admiration and respect he'd garnered. No one here in Pacific Bay seemed to understand. Not even these guys.

"I guess you have a point," Ben told him. "Glad you're in your sweet spot, man. It's just not mine."

Rhett found his beer had grown warm, so he ordered another round.

They spent the next hour catching up. Rhett was happy to hear about Cam and his new life with Allie. Apparently, he'd fallen hard. No one in town really expected he'd ever marry again. But when that cute gal from Texas showed up on the scene, all bets were off. Their wedding had been on the beach. Nearly everyone in town attended.

Ben loved his new baby girl, now nearly a year old. It's all he could talk about, really. Little Rory loved smashed bananas, but hated peas. She loved her bath but didn't like going down at night and often cried. In her daddy's opinion, she was the most beautiful little baby ever.

Ben's face glowed as he provided every detail. Cam and Rhett cut him some slack. He'd been through hell losing his son, and they were really happy to hear life had dealt him a new happiness card...one he truly deserved.

"What about you, Rhett? You say you don't have time for women. Does that mean you've written off hooking up with someone?" Ben asked.

Cam piped in. "Your work sounds great, but the days and nights can get lonely. Take it from me. I pushed the chance for another relationship away for a long time. Losing Julia gut-punched me something awful. I'm glad I took the chance and opened up to the possibility that life could be different. I'm just saying..."

Rhett held up two open palms. "Okay, okay...what is this? An advice-for-the-lovelorn column? Trust me...I've got my life handled. And right now, it doesn't include a woman."

Ben nudged him with an elbow. "I hope you're not telling us you're into something else...something we don't know about?" His face broke into a teasing grin.

"I'm not even justifying that one with an answer." Ignoring his buddy's good-natured jabs, Rhett skipped the mug. Instead, he lifted the beer bottle directly to his lips and took a long draw.

"Hey, did you hear Diane Jeffers is back in town?" Cam mentioned, finishing off his beer.

Rhett leaned and placed his forearms on the table. "That so?"

"Yeah, you remember her," Ben said. "I mean, didn't you have a crush on Diane in school?"

Rhett quickly denied the fact. "Uh, not so. Sure, I thought she was cute. But she was pretty stand-offish, if I remember correctly. And then she up and left town right after high school."

Axel appeared with another round and placed the frosty bottles on the table. He picked up the empties and moved for the bar.

"Well, she's back in town now. She was married to some

politician guy in California who got caught with his pants down around his ankles, so to speak," Cam explained.

"Yeah, created a huge media scandal," Ben added, grabbing his bottle and twisting off the cap.

Rhett slowly nodded. "Oh, yeah. I remember seeing some news stories on television."

Ben shook his head. "You must live under a rock. The news was filled with stories. Toppled the guy's aspirations. Some claimed Richard Park was headed for the White House. Not anymore."

Rhett was sorry to hear that. He'd always liked Diane. He was also sorry to learn she'd left town because she was pregnant. "So, who was the guy?"

Ben looked up. "The guy?"

"Yeah," Rhett said. "Who was the father?"

Cam leaned back in his chair. "Well, hold tight to your beer bottle. She finally revealed Craig Anthony to be the father. Created some town drama for a spell."

"Can't say I ever liked that guy. Arrogant as hell," Ben told them. "Had to be a surprise though, learning he had a teenage daughter."

"Yeah, but he's really stepped up," Cam argued. "From what I hear, he's taken responsibility for the girl and seems to be working hard at building a relationship with her."

Rhett shuddered. "Wow, that must've melted the chips in Mayor Anthony's cookies." His own family dynamics could be challenging. At least he didn't have Barbara Anthony for a mother. "I didn't care for the guy either back in high school. But you have to extend credit to Craig. Sounds like he's trying to do the right thing."

It dawned on Rhett he really was the odd man out. While all his buddies had somehow morphed from footfall jocks into tame family men, he was married to a career. One he loved, but if he was truthful, financial spreadsheets didn't keep a man warm at night. He missed the feel of a woman nestled beside him.

Before he could mentally explore the thought further, his cell phone buzzed in his pocket. He pulled it out. It was Gary Andover. Rhett lifted from the table. "Sorry guys. I've got to take this."

6

Once a year, Wylie and Grace Duvall hosted a festive oyster feed. Everyone in town was invited and looked forward to gathering on the sprawling lawns surrounding the Pacific Bay Oyster Farm operation. The event was a potluck of sorts, with all the women in town bringing their finest dishes.

Carol Deegan could be counted on to bring her beloved parmesan chicken casserole. Bea Followill's marionberry avocado spinach salad with her homemade poppyseed vinaigrette was a favorite, as was Joyce Mintzas's honey butter skillet corn. Then there were the desserts. Jeannette Flores's warm chocolate cobbler was to die for! As was Bambi Rathman's sticky toffee pudding.

The real showstopper, and the main reason for the high annual attendance, was the oysters—baked, fried, poached, and grilled. Some were topped with decadent cheeses from the Tillamook cheese factory, some had a splash of pepper sauce and butter melted on top with lots of garlic, and no one could count all the shucked oysters eaten fresh from the shell. But all were consumed in record time as soon as the platters were placed on the long tables.

This year, the party coincided with Wylie's birthday, his big seventy-fifth. Grace and the entire family were pulling out all the stops. Nothing in the past, and likely nothing in the future, would ever compete.

Grace bent to the kitchen floor and opened a large box with one of her kitchen paring knives. "Rhett, honey. Could you help me hang these strings of lights?"

"Mom, we hired people to do that. Remember?"

She waved off his comment. "Oh, I know. But there's so much. I thought we could get a head start this morning."

Rhett grinned and gently took hold of her arm, pulled her aside. "You've spent weeks preparing for this event. Everything is in order. Now, your job is simply to relax and let everyone else finish what needs to be done. Try and enjoy the day."

His mother looked at him like he had two heads. "We both know things can go wrong at the last minute."

He kissed the top of her blonde head. "Which is why I'm here. I'll take care of everything, make sure nothing goes awry."

His mother smiled back at him, patted his arm. "You've always been my little fixer."

It was true. He often found himself in the role of cleaning up problems, resurrecting failed plans, and ensuring everything went smoothly. Life was less complicated if you took control and didn't always depend on others who might let you down.

The door opened, and his sister called out, "Hey, guys. We're here."

Billy and Levi darted into the kitchen, both wrapping their little arms around his legs and nearly toppling him in the process. "Uncle Wet!"

Rhett grinned and pried himself free. "Hey, guys. You up for the big birthday party?"

Levi, the littlest one, nodded. His eyes grew wide. "Yessir, we even have presents for Papa. But Grammy says we have to keep that a secret."

"Yes, you do," Grace confirmed. She turned to her daughter and winked. "We'll see how well that works."

Wes sauntered into the kitchen, rubbing his generous belly. "Hey, you got anything to eat?" He leaned and kissed his mother-in-law's cheek.

Leila popped her husband on the arm. "You already had breakfast." She turned to her mom. "He had four pancakes and a half-pound of bacon."

"That was hours ago," Wes complained.

"Excuse me, but that was just before we left the house," Leila corrected. She placed a bag loaded with party items on the counter. "Everything is coming together outside, Mom. I ordered fifty oblong tables. Do you think we'll need more chairs?"

Rhett poured himself another cup of coffee. "Got it handled," he said, shutting off the coffee maker. "I called. The rental company is bringing three dozen additional seats to be left in the truck. They'll unload them immediately if we find we need them."

"Where's Pop?" Leila asked, peering out the window.

His mother wiped her hands on her apron. "He got up early and went into town to mail some packages. He promised he'd be back in plenty of time to shower before all the activity starts."

Rhett's father was sun-kissed and solid from spending a lifetime outside. Hours from now, he'd be overseeing the grilling and barking orders to those pulling the baked oysters from the pit where they'd been buried in soaked burlap bags over twelve hours before. He'd pay no attention to the fact this party was being thrown to honor him. He was always at his happiest while serving the people of the community he called home.

Rhett joined his mother, and together, they made their way outside. White tablecloths were being draped over the last of the tables. Strings of lights had been strung from tree limbs, and the local florist was positioning mason jars filled with brightly colored dahlias.

His mom clasped her hands together. "Oh, my! Everything looks absolutely perfect."

Rhett placed his arm around her shoulder and gave a tight squeeze. "See? Nothing to worry about."

He scanned the area for any sign of Jared. Both the oyster operation and the retail store were shut down for the day—a rare decision, but a necessary one. His mother was insistent she wanted all the workers free to join them. Given that, his brother should be up at the house helping out. He was about to mention the fact when Jared's pickup rounded the bend and pulled into the shell-packed driveway.

Grace waved in his direction. "Your brother's been running errands for me since the crack of dawn. Such a big help." She bent to pluck a weed from the lawn. "I don't know what we'd have done without him these past months."

Rhett swallowed, hating how hard that was to hear. Not that he wasn't glad his brother was finally paying back his parents for some of what he'd put them through, but there was a saying that kept playing in his head. *The higher you climb, the harder the fall.* No doubt, that fall would eventually come. It always did. Unfortunately, his parents would be the ones to suffer the brunt of Jared's tumble.

"Hey, Mom," Jared said as he approached carrying a box.

Rhett scowled. "What's that?"

His mom parked her hands inside the box and started counting. "Electrical cords. Remember how we ran out last year?" Satisfied with her count, she shook her head. "Last year we ran out when it suddenly got hot, and we wanted to set up some of the fans."

That made Rhett laugh. "Well, we have a great breeze today. Doubt we'll run into that issue."

Jared carried the box over and set it down next to racks filled with wine glasses. "Hey, Mom. I think I saw Pop's truck in town."

Grace's face filled with concern. "Oh? Where was he?"

"The Pig 'n' Pancake."

Leila's boys raced across the lawn. Billy held a hose and was spraying his younger brother.

Grace's hands flew up. "Boys! Stop that! You're going to get everything all wet."

The door into the house flew open, and out came Leila, followed by Wes holding a leftover piece of fried chicken to his mouth. "Billy! Levi! Get over here. Now!"

Jared scooped his keys from his pocket. "I'm going to head back in and check on Pop," he said.

Grace wiped her brow with her forearm and nodded.

"Check on him?" Rhett asked.

Grace and Jared exchanged glances. "You know your father," his mom quickly explained. "He'll get to talking with the boys and lose track of time."

Jared turned and started walking.

"I'll go with you," Rhett said.

"No. That's all right. I got this," he said firmly over his shoulder.

Rhett ignored the remark and followed him anyway. "We'll be back soon, Mom."

It had been a long while since Rhett had enjoyed a meal at the Pig 'n' Pancake. In high school, the popular café, known for its breakfasts, was one of his favorite haunts. He especially loved the huckleberry pancakes. The place was owned by his pal's dad, Muncy Davis. Because of his friendship with Cal,

Muncy had often thrown in a plate of crispy fried bacon for free.

At least that's how things used to be. Rhett glanced over at his brother as he parked his truck. Seems a lot of things had changed.

Rhett climbed from the pickup and glanced around. Even at this early hour, the area was already bustling with people anxious to visit the art galleries and restaurants along the wharf. Rhett and Jared made their way past street boxes filled with bright yellow and orange mums and to the front door. A little bell rang as Jared opened it, and they stepped inside.

"Hey, Pop," Jared said, moving in the direction of their dad who sat on a swivel stool at the counter holding a mug of coffee in his hand.

Muncy wiped the counter with a bar towel. "Hey, boys." His eyes grew soft. "Welcome home, Rhett. Your dad was just telling me you were back for a visit. You're looking good." He came from around the counter and pulled him into a tight embrace. "So, can I get you boys something to eat? Some pancakes?" He scrubbed at a speck of dried food he noticed was stuck on the worn speckled surface.

"Nah," Jared told him. "Mom wanted us to come check on Pop." He placed his hand on his dad's shoulder. "She's got a bunch left for us to do, ole' man. You know how she gets on party day."

Wylie placed his hand behind his ear as if he were deaf. "Come again. Grace is throwing a party?"

Muncy flipped the towel over his shoulder and straightened the plastic menus in the silver rack mounted at the edge of the counter. "Your big birthday party, Wylie. Gonna be quite the bash, I hear. Bigger than ever before, and that's saying something."

Wylie turned confused. He scratched at the fringe of gray-white hair around his balding mottled scalp. "It's my...my birthday?"

That's when Rhett saw it. An immediate sliver of panic raced down his spine.

His dad seemed...lost. There could be no other word to describe the confused look in his father's eyes as he turned to face his sons.

Rhett cut a glance to Jared. His brother quickly looked away. He squeezed their father's shoulder. "Let's go, Pop. It's an important day."

7

Rhett drove his dad's pickup, seething. In front of him, Jared's truck held his brother and father. Their pop had argued initially, but finally consented to Jared driving him home under the ruse of needing to discuss some important business matters.

Something was definitely up with their dad, and his brother was hiding whatever it was. Rhett could put up with his brother needling back into his parents' favor. He'd pushed back a trickle of resentment when he learned Jared was now hanging with his own friends. When learning his wayward brother was now making business decisions and advising his folks on matters of importance, he'd simply gritted his teeth and kept his mouth shut. Hiding an issue with their dad's health was not acceptable. Make no mistake, Jared was going to hear about it.

His phone buzzed.

Rhett reached across the seat and grabbed it. He groaned upon noticing the call was coming in from Judith Sandidge, his boss.

He pulled the phone to his ear. "Hey, Judy."

"When is your flight back?" she asked, not bothering with a

greeting. "Everything with the Markowitz Herbold deal is blowing up. I need you back here holding Harry Markowitz's hand. You're the one he trusts."

Rhett's mind raced. "I—I'll see what I can do." His thoughts immediately went to what had just transpired with his pop and mentally calculated the risk of staying a few days. "Don't worry, Judy. I'll get on a video conference with him and—"

"Harry is old. He hates technology." She paused, letting the gravity of the situation sink in. "I don't need to tell you how important this deal is to the firm. We're counting on you, Rhett."

"There's no need to worry," he promised. "I won't let you down."

As he hung up, he realized he might need an act of the Almighty to juggle everything before him. No way could he leave and return home without understanding the full story on what was going on with his dad. It was dawning on him that he was out of the loop, had been kept in the dark—perhaps on purpose.

The fact rankled him to no end that his mother trusted Jared with information about their father's health but hadn't bothered to include their only son who had proven himself committed to … well, *anything* for more than half a second.

The minute they arrived back at the house, Rhett turned off the engine and burst from the car. He made his way to Jared and grabbed his arm. With his voice lowered, he barely bothered to hide the anger building inside. "Hey, bro. I need to talk to you."

Out of the corner of his eye, Rhett saw his mother waving them over.

He gave his brother's arm a slight tug. "I'm not kidding. Now."

Jared pulled away. "Hey, lighten up."

"Now," Rhett repeated, using the big brother tone he used

to employ in high school when he caught an underaged Jared out drinking with his buddies or passed out in the back seat of his car in the high school parking lot.

"There you are," Rhett's mom said, eyeing the situation as she joined them. She threaded her hand in her husband's. Rhett couldn't help but notice the way her gaze stalled for a moment on Jared. Something passed between them. She blinked it away and patted her husband's forearm. "Where were you, darling? Did you forget all that we had to do to get ready for your big day?"

His pop leaned and kissed her cheek. "No, Mama. I didn't forget. I just got caught up in conversation over a pancake or two. That's all."

Rhett watched his father closely. His eyes shifted from Rhett's mom to Jared, the slightest of frowns creasing his brow. It appeared he, too, was covering the situation up to some extent. Could no one admit what was becoming apparent? Even his nephew had clued in that his dad was having memory issues. He needed to get to the bottom of this.

"Let's go inside," Rhett told Jared, with a look that warned not to cross him.

Jared and his mother exchanged another wary glance before she wrapped her arm around her husband's waist, gave a squeeze. "C'mon, birthday boy. No more lollygagging. We have to help get that pit ready for the oyster bake." As she led their father slowly away, she glanced back at them over her shoulder. No doubt, she understood Rhett was no longer in the dark.

"Let's have it," he demanded as soon as he and Jared were inside the house.

"Ssh...calm down," Jared warned. "You don't need to tip off an explosion here." He motioned for their father's office. "In here."

Rhett followed him to the familiar room where he'd spent so many hours with his pop, learning the business and all the facets of oyster farming. He'd learned to read a profit and loss statement sitting at that worn desk. His father had drummed the risks of overextending one's credit and how to manage cash flow while sitting in the worn leather desk chair. In so many ways, those moments seemed like just yesterday.

His father had always been larger than life, the solid rock in the family. Rhett now realized he wasn't...well, he might not be the superhuman Rhett had thought.

"Okay, look. Pop's been having a few challenges," Jared explained. "But the doctor up in Astoria said—"

"The doctor?" Rhett's heart squeezed. He frowned and shook his head, confused.

"He's having memory issues, Rhett."

The words felt like anchors pulling him under. Despite his stoic nature, a sliver of terror ran down his spine. "What do you mean, memory issues?"

Jared placed his hand on his brother's shoulder. "Don't freak out. The doctor up in Astoria said that some memory loss is not all that unusual for someone his age."

Rhett shrugged away. He pulled his hand across the top of his hair in frustration. "Seventy-five is not old, Jared. You felt like he needed medical evaluation, but didn't tell me?"

Jared held up open palms, trying to halt the onslaught of Rhett's questions. "See? This is what we were afraid of."

"We?" The world slowed to a crawl as the implication sunk in. "Who exactly is *we*?"

"Mom, Leila—"

Rhett didn't let him finish. "You couldn't pick up the phone and call me? What the—I mean, I'm part of this family, in case you didn't remember. Who do you think you are, unilaterally making the decision to exclude me? He's my father, too, you know."

Jared motioned between them. "This. This is why we were reluctant to call you, Rhett. This is what you do. You throw a fit if you don't have all the information. You pummel everyone with questions, demanding answers. You step in and take over, often without regard for anyone else's wishes or feelings. You're like a bulldozer."

Rhett clenched his fists so tightly they hurt. "You little punk. After everything you've done? All that you've put Mom and Pop through, you think you have the right to lecture *me*?" He pounded his fist to the desktop. "You've got to be kidding!"

The door flew open, and in strode their mother. "Boys! We can hear you two clear out in the yard." She extended her arms between them almost as if she believed they might come to blows. "This is not the time."

She focused on Rhett. "Your father is fine. He— Well, he simply gets a little tired now and again and his memory slips a bit. That's all." She lowered her gaze and brushed imaginary lint from her dress, her words dropping to a whisper. "There was no reason to trouble you."

Rhett looked at her with disappointment. "You, too?"

His mother's back stiffened. She lifted her chin and pinned him with a sharp look. "Son, we will have this discussion later. But not now. Today is your father's birthday. We have guests coming and I'm not going to allow anything to ruin his special day." She pointed her finger at Rhett for emphasis. "Understood?" She gave her younger son a light pat on the back. "Now, c'mon. Let's all go celebrate your father's birthday."

The air left Rhett's lungs. In a strange reversal, she was chastising him and not Jared. In his absence, his brother had apparently become the favorite. He'd managed to become the shoulder their mother leaned on—the one his mother counted on, confided in. Surely, she understood her trust was misplaced.

He opened his mouth to argue the point, but his mother had already moved for the door. Without looking back, she turned the knob and marched out.

Rhett took a deep breath and folded his arms across his chest, not letting that throw him. He looked over at Jared. "This isn't over." He paused and turned for the door, trying and failing to ignore the sinking sensation unfurling in his gut. He swallowed the thickness in his throat and muttered under his breath, "Not by a long shot."

8

Outside, the driveway was now filled with trucks and cars. People had been arriving over the past hour, and the party was about to get underway. The band was tuning up their instruments under his mom's gazebo and the aromas of cooking food could be detected even inside the house. While the rest of his family had showered and dressed and were now out greeting guests, Rhett buried himself in his pop's office in front of the computer.

In less than an hour, Rhett had educated himself on the onset of dementia, learned about the major symptoms of Alzheimer's disease, and what all that could mean. While overwhelmed with the load of information available, all of which he would eventually study carefully, it was apparent that it was good that he was home. He tried to tell himself his family meant well, that they simply did not want to alarm him. Yet no one was better equipped to take all this on. His pop needed the best medical care, evaluation by a dedicated team of professionals who were experts in this field. He would make sure that would happen.

Rhett let out a deep breath and powered the computer

down, then hurried upstairs to clean up. After a quick shower, he pulled on a pair of chinos and a button-down shirt. He splashed some cologne on his neck and then joined his family for the birthday festivities, determined to put his dad's health concerns aside, at least for a little while.

By the time Rhett stepped outside onto the back deck, the party was in full swing. Party attendees gathered in small clusters across the sprawling lawn, chatting. He recognized many. Susan Wilson, the owner of the garden shop in town was smiling as some ladies complimented the table florals. Dr. Pierard, the town veterinarian sauntered over and accepted a glass of freshly poured beer from Pete Lennon. Pete always helped out at the keg and knew the fine art of pouring some draft with just the right amount of foam. Axel, the bartender down at the Sea Star Tavern, looked over his shoulder and offered a few unsolicited pointers.

A bus from the Ebb Tide Retirement Home pulled up. The doors opened and the driver provided assistance to several of the residents by helping them exit, then helped them get settled in their wheelchairs and positioned with their walkers.

Linda Pullen strode across the lawn, carrying a massive birthday cake. She owned the Bayfront Bakery, and year after year argued with his mother over accepting payment for her contribution to the event.

Rhett got a bottle of his favorite craft beer of his own from the cooler nearby and then headed in the direction of the roasting pit lined with racks of oysters covered with damp burlap. Several men huddled around the brick-lined pit, waiting with knives in hand, ready for a go at a steaming pile of large Kumamotos that had been freshly harvested that morning.

"Hey, bud," Cam greeted him with a tip of his long neck beer bottle. "Where you been?"

Rhett gave him a congenial pat on the back. "Just had some things I had to attend to."

Sam Marcum, the cook down at the Pig 'n' Pancake, wagged a pair of stainless-steel tongs in his direction. "Your folks say you work entirely too much. Work hard? Yes. But don't forget to play harder!" He laughed as he moved some cooked oysters onto platters and handed them off into Thelma Kennedy's dimpled hands.

The heavy woman nodded in agreement. "Come on down to the Legion Hall tomorrow night. We're going to have a rousing game of Bingo. It'd do you good to have some fun."

Rhett thanked her and promised he would consider her offer.

She leaned close. "There's a lot of pretty young girls sitting at those Bingo tables. You just never know. You might find your future wife holding a dauber in her hand." She winked and waddled away, chuckling to herself.

His friend, Ben, approached. "What's everybody laughing about?"

Cam grinned. "Thelma is trying to hook Rhett up."

"And, I'm not laughing," Rhett injected. "While I may marry someday, it's not likely to be to anyone from Pacific Bay—or, anyone Thelma would choose."

"Oh?" Olivia Arrington stepped next to them, holding a cute toddler against her hip. "What's wrong with the women from Pacific Bay?"

Rhett granted her a wide smile. "Nothing. It's just that all the good ones are taken." He leaned and kissed her cheek. "So, this is the little one?" He looked over at Ben. "Dang, you're one lucky guy, Arrington."

"Yeah, I am," Ben conceded and took the baby from her mother. "Even with the two a.m. wake-up-to-play issue we have going on right now."

Olivia gave her husband a playful slap on the forearm.

"Okay, mister. You started it." She leaned over with her hand at the side of her mouth, speaking in a conspiratorial manner. "Ben used to get up to feed her and instead of putting our daughter right back down, he entertained her by zooming Rory around the nursery like Superwoman. In the middle of the night!" She shook her head. "No complaining. You did this yourself, dada."

Ben shrugged and nuzzled his nose against his baby girl's, causing her to quake with baby laughter. "I don't remember doing that." His daughter gurgled and rested her head against Ben's strong shoulder.

Olivia laughed and pulled Aurora from Ben's arms. "You hang with the guys. I'm going to check and see if Grace needs any help." She looked at Rhett. "Your mom is amazing."

He agreed with her. Across the lawn, he could see his mother buzzing around, making sure everyone had plenty to eat and drink. As soon as someone's plate emptied, she'd wave over one of the servers and load them back up with oysters and ears of corn, dripping with garlic butter. While he was too far away to actually hear, she was no doubt saying, "Eat. And there's plenty more where that came from."

Rhett excused himself and sauntered over to the food tables, realizing his own stomach was now growling. With everything that had transpired this morning, he'd neglected to eat breakfast or lunch.

In addition to baked oysters pulled from the roasting pit, there were platters of fresh fried oysters from the fryers. Piles of bacon-wrapped smoked oysters bordered an array of crackers. Just past those, soup tureens filled with oyster stew awaited.

Rhett grabbed a plate and scooped a general helping of each. He filled a cup with some stew and made his way to an empty place at a table near the water's edge. "This seat taken?" he asked.

Pastor Riggin looked up, smiled, and shook his head. "No,

please join us." He motioned for him to sit. "Welcome home, Rhett. Glad to see you're back for a visit." Then, motioning to the teenagers sitting at the table with him, he said, "You remember Nolan?"

A young kid with tousled brown hair grinned back at him, a large shell suspended in one hand and an oyster knife poised in the other. "Hey."

Rhett set his plate down before extending a hand. He turned to the girl sitting next to Nolan. "I don't believe we've met," Rhett said as he slid into his seat.

Pastor Riggin picked up his fork. "This is Nolan's friend. Stacy," he said, making introductions. "Stacy, this is Rhett Duvall. This is his folks' place, and they're the hosts of this big celebration." The white-haired pastor scooped up some potato salad. "I've known Rhett since he was a toddler."

It was true. Rhett had clear memories of spending Sunday mornings at New Hope Church sitting on a hard, wooden pew next to his mother. He'd been told to sit still during the service, and any time he made a transgression, she'd give him *the look*. If he was stupid enough to ignore that initial warning, his actions earned him a quick knuckle thump to the head.

While his memories of church were not always stellar, Pastor Riggin was one of the best dudes in town. Everyone in Pacific Bay respected him. He was one of those who actually lived out what he preached. The guy was kind and generous, always putting service to others far before his own needs. It was no surprise to anyone when he took in a young kid who had been abandoned by his mother at age three. Without a second thought, Pastor Riggin raised him and had given him a home.

"Stacy is Ellen Jeffers's granddaughter," Pastor Riggin told him. "I think you went to school with her mother?"

Rhett nodded. "Ah, yes. I heard Diane moved back," he said, taking a spoon to the bowl of oyster stew.

Stacey made a face. "You like that stuff?"

He laughed. "Yeah, why?"

The young girl shrugged. "I dunno. It looks a little like globs floating in milk." Her nose scrunched at the thought.

Nolan gave her shoulder a playful nudge with his. "Ah, c'mon. You're not afraid to try it, are you?" He scooped up some in a spoon and held it to her mouth.

Rhett could tell she wanted to argue. She glanced at the bowl, then back up at Nolan and the challenge written on his face. Bracing herself, she opened her mouth and took the offered bite. Her eyes immediately went wide. "Not bad," she exclaimed. "I mean, pretty good, actually."

"Yeah, what's not to like?" Nolan asked. "This soup is made with cream and butter, celery and onions. And oysters, of course. I'll have to show you how to fix the recipe sometime."

She nodded with enthusiasm. "Okay, sure. But first, I want to learn how to make Oysters Rockefeller. Now, these are really delicious!" She slipped one inside her mouth and smiled with pleasure.

"Hey, is this who I think it is?" a female voice rang out.

Rhett turned to find Diane Jeffers standing with her hands on her hips, grinning. His own face sprouted a smile as she moved for him and drew him into a hug. "Goodness, what's it been?" She quickly waved her comment off. "Never mind. Don't answer. It'll only make me feel old."

"You are definitely not old. Because I'm not. Old, that is." He motioned for her to sit with them, and she slid into the empty chair across from him.

Diane's eyes sparkled with little flecks of gold. She looked... good. No, amazing. Amazingly good. Rhett cleared his throat, hoping no one noticed how his gaze lingered on her. She was—after all—off-limits. Fresh from a very public and messy divorce and also a Pacific Bay girl. And Rhett wasn't staying.

Rhett shook off the thought and gave his attention back to Diane. "Can I get you something to eat?" he offered.

"Oh, no. I already snuck a few of the oysters they were pulling off the grill. I'm stuffed," she told him.

"And she's watching her weight," her daughter teased.

"Careful," her mother warned. "I know a lot of your secrets, too, you know."

Pastor Riggin rubbed his own belly. "I'm watching my weight, too. I've watched this belly expand for years now." He laughed, as did everyone else at the table.

"So, Cam and Ben told me you'd moved back," Rhett said, going for another bite of stew. "From Los Angeles?"

She nodded. "Yes, a rather long story. I'm back. And, I'm truly surprised how much I enjoy living back in Pacific Bay."

Nolan scraped the last bite from his plate. "You ready for some dessert?" he asked Stacey.

Pastor Riggin lifted from the table, his now empty plate in hand. "Heard they had some homemade marionberry ice cream. Who's in?"

Stacey grinned. "Twist my arm!" She looked over at her mother as she gathered her things from the table and followed Pastor Riggin and Nolan from the table. "Despite what Mom says, I plan on not watching my weight until tomorrow."

"Oh, to be that young again," her mother said, sighing. "She makes fun of me for counting calories, but she won't stay looking pencil-thin forever. Trust me on that."

Rhett wanted to argue that point. Diane looked nearly the same as she had in high school. She was gorgeous then, and she still was. He was no stranger to beautiful women, but he was often one who judged a woman by her eyes. You could tell a lot about a person from their eyes.

Diane's were deep brown, the color of expensive chocolate. She had thick lashes, fine, thin, arching brows, and that golden sparkle that begged him to keep looking. Those eyes reflected humor, curiosity, and intelligence.

He remembered how smart she was in school. Back then,

she could prove algebraic equations far better than anyone else. He'd struggled with abstract computations. Over the years, he'd learned and was now an expert at using matrix equations, rank and null space to examine financial conditions. Still, he might never have passed algebra class without her as his assigned study partner. He told her so now.

She threw her head back and laughed. "That's right. If I remember correctly, you offered to take me to prom if I'd do your assignments."

He laughed, too. "And you told me just what I could do with that suggestion."

She covered her face with her hands. "Oh, goodness. I didn't!"

He nodded with enthusiasm. "Oh, yes. You most certainly did."

Out of habit, his eyes went to her hand to look for rings. Did she still wear hers? Some women did after the divorce if they didn't want to ward off men who were looking. Then he remembered the nastiness of the news stories and what the guys had told him about her strong right hook. Nope. No rings there.

Looking like she sensed what he was thinking, she brought the subject up. "So, I guess you heard I'm no longer married." They both knew how news spreads in small towns. "And why."

He nodded in sympathy. "Yeah, I heard. I'm so sorry, Diane. That's rough."

She recited the whole embarrassing situation, how her husband got embroiled in a sexual scandal during his senatorial campaign. She'd been naïve enough to support him, until she discovered the allegations were true.

"I'm afraid I lost my mind a little. Acted very unbecoming," she admitted. "Of course, it was all caught on camera."

"From what I hear, he deserved it," Rhett told her. "Besides, what's over is over. All of us have something in our backgrounds we'd shed, if possible."

"Yeah? Don't tell me." Her voice held a teasing tone. "You ran a Ponzi scheme and lost all your clients' money. Now, they're all mad, so you ran home to Pacific Bay to hide out."

That made Rhett laugh. "Nah, most of us in the financial and investment community learned from Bernie Madoff how that plays out."

"So, do you like living in Chicago?" She leaned forward, lowered her voice. "Admittedly, I do miss the big city on occasion. The stores, the lights, the buzz of—well, of life. It's much quieter here."

"I can imagine. And yes, I do like Chicago. For all the reasons you stated, but I like the fact that I can walk out my door and go for a run and never run into a single soul I know. No making chit-chat, no trying to remember so-and-so's niece's name and where she's currently going to college. Know what I mean?"

Her eyes now filled with laughter. "I know exactly what you mean."

Cam and Allie headed in their direction. "Hey, you guys being unsocial?" Allie asked as they neared.

"Not at all," Rhett told her. "Join us."

Cam set their loaded plates on the table. Allie placed a glass of red wine down and slipped in the chair beside her husband. "I've been looking forward to this for months. And your dad? Well, he sure doesn't look like he's seventy-five."

"He works circles around most men in town," Cam said, tucking a napkin on his lap and eyeing the contents of his plate. "He deserves to slow down some. Jared seems to be stepping up, and that should allow Wylie to step away some. Maybe he can even board a jet and come for a visit—huh, Rhett?"

Rhett's mood quickly soured. "Well, yeah—Pop is going to have to slow down." That time might be sooner than later.

Somehow, he couldn't bring himself to reveal the entirety of his concern just yet. He swallowed hard against the ache in his chest. "When that happens, Jared isn't capable of taking over this operation. Oh, sure, he may know the oyster beds and harvesting aspects of this business, but the international marketing and the financial end of things—well, that extends well past his current capability."

Allie gave him a nod, her expression sympathetic. "I remember when I first took over Uncle Tarver's fishing charter. I was so over my head." She turned to Cam. "Wasn't I, honey?"

"Yes," Cam said, agreeing with her. "But you quickly learned and created a thriving business."

Allie smiled. "I did. I guess a person can do almost anything prompted by necessity. And with a little help from friends."

Cam scooped up a bite of Spud Murphy's famous coleslaw. "Jared may have a lot to learn, Rhett, but your brother is fully dedicated to your folks. And we're all here to support him. I think he'll do just fine."

Rhett scowled, wanting to argue. He appreciated Cam and Allie's positive assessment of the situation, but they didn't know his brother like he did. Jared was the last person who could be trusted to run an operation that would provide the necessary retirement funds for his parents. As soon as word got out, and it soon would, about his father's mental health decline and the serious nature of what might be ahead, Cam and Allie would have to agree with him. No responsible person would ever place his folks' financial security in the hands of someone who had a long pattern of flaking out when it was important. There was simply too much at stake.

The notion his brother had hidden from him the fact his father was facing mental health issues and had convinced the family to go along with that secrecy—well, that said everything, right there. If that was a sign of his brother's stellar judgment, no further argument needed to be made.

No way would Rhett leave his parents' future in Jared's hands. No one would. Sure, Jared may be finally changing his life around, even making a few better choices, but in Rhett's opinion, the turn-around was a bit too little, too late. And who was to say his self-redemption would last?

Despite his own full plate, Rhett would simply have to find a way to step in and right this ship before his father and everything he'd worked for all these years crashed on shore.

9

The following morning, everyone was in serious clean-up mode. With his mother at the helm, the entire family rose from bed just after dawn and joined many of the farmworkers outside. There were tents to take down, tables to load back into trucks, and strings of lights to wind and store until they'd use them again next year. Vendors from town arrived on the scene and retrieved the beer kegs, the extra tables and chairs and chafing dishes they'd used to keep the food at safe temperatures.

Leonard, the local trash man, agreed to make a special run to haul away a pile of garbage bags filled with post-party refuse. Rhett's nephews were handed rakes, and while they were young, their grandmother tasked them with raking up all the shells that somehow made their way into the grass. Leila helped his mom with kitchen duty. Despite hiring most of the catering, there was still a pile of dirty dishes remaining to be washed, dried, and put away.

Rhett peeked inside the back door that served as an entrance to the kitchen. "Hey, Mom," he said. "Looks like the clean-up effort is wrapping up. Do you need anything else?"

"No, honey. Leila and I are going to finish up here, and then I'll heat up that coffee cake Linda Pullen left for us. You might go check on your father and brother."

"Sure thing, Mom." Rhett wandered out to the main packing shed where his brother ran the boom as a dinghy was loaded with spat trays. The process was being overseen by their father.

"Hey, Pop," Rhett said, patting his old man on the shoulder. "That was some party last night. I'm not sure Mom is going to be able to top that one for some time to come."

His dad pulled a handkerchief from his overalls and wiped his brow. "Yeah, she gets a big kick out of putting on those parties."

Rhett agreed. "Not sure what the final count might have been, but I doubt very much there were but a few in town who missed it. Everyone wanted to come out and wish you happy birthday."

His pop gave him one of those side grins, the ones that sprouted on his face when he was about to tell a joke. He opened his mouth to say something and paused. It was as if what he was about to say got lost.

Rhett felt his breath catch. "You okay, Pop?"

His father straightened. "Yeah, sure. Why wouldn't I be?" He pointed to the boom. "Best check to see if your brother needs some help getting those trays loaded."

Rhett nodded and reluctantly moved to join Jared. He climbed carefully into the boat with the other workers, now wishing he'd thought to pull on his rubber boots. The deck was slimy in spots, and he didn't want to slip and land on his backside. The workers all considered him a city slicker, and he didn't care to do anything to cement the notion.

Few of the current workers would remember that he'd lived on this oyster farm. He was the one who weighed and raised spat in the old lantern nets, the one who waded into the shore grasses and worked the longlines with a six-foot davit with a horizontal reach of only two feet.

He wasn't the sort to brag, but he knew this operation better than anyone. The fact he didn't live on the oyster farm anymore didn't mean he'd forgotten how to run this place. Moreover, he'd graduated into the financial side of things, guided his father carefully into the international markets. He'd cautiously divested their earnings, investing in high-profit stocks with margins that made strong men weep with joy.

The profit generated provided the funds for necessary renovations. Equipment didn't last forever. Building a digital sales platform and updating the website had also taken significant funds. Running an operation of this size wasn't cheap.

No one could argue Rhett was an integral part of the backbone of this family operation. His father knew it. Sure, he'd been bringing his younger son up to speed recently, but Pop knew who he could count on to protect Pacific Bay Oyster Farm, a business that had been passed down through multiple generations. Just because he'd moved to Chicago didn't mean he had abdicated helping out when necessary.

When they were finished loading the spat trays onto the boat, Rhett grabbed some towels from a hook in the shed, and cleared the muck from his shoes and wiped his hands. He quietly asked the tumbling foreman to keep his dad busy for a while. Back inside the house, he called a family meeting.

"Rhett, honey. Don't you think you're overreacting a bit?" his mother suggested while taking her seat at the dining table. Across the table sat his sister, Leila. She dipped her tea bag in a cup of hot water. "I hope this will be quick. The kids will get surly if they miss story hour down at the library."

Rhett assured them what he had to say wouldn't take long.

"How long is long?" Wes asked. He cut a large piece of the coffee cake and put it on a paper plate. "I want to get home in time to watch the game."

Rhett had to bite his lip to keep from spouting a retort. Had they all included him from the start, this little family conversation might not be necessary. Years in corporate America had taught him to keep those kinds of thoughts to himself. There was only one thing he needed to accomplish, and that was to inform his family that now that he was aware of their father's mental health issue, he was in charge.

Of course, it wouldn't be politically correct to word it quite that bluntly. This is where the art of persuasion would come into play. "I know we're all tired and have things to do. The sooner we get started, the sooner we'll be done."

While not happy about it, his brother-in-law grabbed his coffee cake, a bag of chips, and a couple of sodas and took the boys outside to play.

"Look, I appreciate you all indulging me here," Rhett began when he finally had their full attention. "We're a family, and we're on the same team. You're all aware I was not happy that you chose not to tell me that Pop was suffering some memory issues, that you sought medical care without consulting me, but that's behind us. What we need to focus on is the future."

Distracted, Leila looked out the window. "Oh, just a minute." She rose from her spot at the table, went to the door, and opened it. "Wes, stop him from eating those worms, will you?" she yelled. "You have to watch him."

Rhett could see Wes lick his fingers and set the open bag of chips down on the ground. He moved for Levi, who proudly held up a fistful of earthworms.

Leila shook her head and shut the door. "Sorry."

Rhett sighed with frustration. "Okay, can we get on with it now?"

Leila shrugged and slid back into her seat at the table. "Sure, go ahead."

"Again, I don't want to take up a bunch of time. I just want you to know that I've done some substantial research." He pulled a stack of printed papers out of the briefcase at his feet. "What we're dealing with here is nothing to fool around about."

Their mom and Jared exchanged glances. Notably, his mom wouldn't make eye contact with Rhett.

"Dementia has stages. From everything I've recently learned and seen, Pop has moderate cognitive decline. He has difficulty concentrating, has some memory deficiencies—"

Leila scowled at him. "Gee, we could follow a little better if you'd just talk in plain English."

Annoyed, Rhett rubbed his temples. "What I'm saying in plain language is that we need to have Pop assessed."

"We did that," Jared argued.

"Oh, honey," his mother inserted. "I know you're only trying to help, but Jared's right. We took your father to a doctor. Yes, he's getting a little forgetful here and there. But Dr. Cannon says that's part of the aging process. Your dad's been under a lot of stress lately. Jared is working to relieve him of worry and let him take things a bit easier."

Rhett bristled inside. He was well aware Jared was the family savior in their eyes. Nevertheless, this issue had been mishandled. "Look, Pop needs to be evaluated by a specialist, someone who understands dementia and—"

His mother scooted her chair back abruptly and stood. "Your father does not have dementia."

Jared stood as well. "Look, bro. You're upsetting her. Let's just can this for now."

Rhett couldn't help but pull his fists into tight balls. Why was it so difficult to make his family see what was right in front of their faces? Was he the only one who could step back and assess the situation objectively? Plan and take the proper steps?

He held up his hands in surrender. "Okay, yeah. Sure. I've said my piece."

A look of relief crossed his mother's face. She gave him a slight smile. "Well, let's make the best of the time you have left.

I don't want to waste a minute of your visit." She turned to Leila. "Now that we've got this party behind us, let's plan some fun. How about a family fishing trip? Call that nice Allie Barrett and see if her vessel is available and book us for in the morning, will you?" She gathered the cups and glasses from the table and moved for the sink.

Leila looked between her brothers. She pushed her chair back. "Sure, Mom. I'll have to find someone to watch the boys. Maybe Olivia Arrington could keep them for the morning."

"Oh, honey," their mom said. "They can come too. It's a family outing." She gave Rhett a directed look. "Something we don't get to do often. Let's make some Duvall memories, shall we?"

Without saying anything more, Jared ran a hand through the top of his hair and headed for the door.

Rhett realized then that he would not have his family's support. His mother was in denial about Pop and what was going on with him. Perhaps it was simply too much for her to accept the idea that her husband of over forty years was facing a future no one would want to embrace. As usual, Leila was distracted and not on board with anything that included conflict. Jared? Well, there was little excuse for his brother's lack of concern. He should know better. Perhaps his wayward brother could remain sober by going to meetings and laying his soul bare in front of strangers, by believing life could be taken one day at a time, or whatever mantra he used to get by, but that wasn't real life.

Real life was a journey. You had to be willing to pack up and go where it took you. He did have one thing in common with his family. He loved and respected Pop, and he wanted what was best for him. Unfortunately, he was the only one in the family who was brave enough to look at this situation clearly, the only member of this family who would do the necessary research and make a plan of action that made sense—staying focused and with all emotion set aside.

That is just what he intended. He'd do the right thing by Pop.

With or without them.

10

After the meeting, Rhett immediately retreated to his father's office. He stood beside the desk holding his pile of research. With renewed determination, he set the papers down on the desk surface and ruffled through until he found the information he'd collected from the Brain Institute at Oregon Health Sciences University website. From what he'd read, there was an entire team of providers and researchers on staff who specialized in frontotemporal dementia and related disorders.

By far, the most highly regarded neurologist on the OHSU team was Dr. Randall Michaels. Dr. Michaels had studied under Dr. Nathan Emerson at the Institute of Brain Sciences in Texas. When Dr. Emerson left his practice to pursue politics, Dr. Michaels became the nation's go-to specialist for brain disorders. His qualifications were impressive, and his writings extensive. He'd even testified before a congressional panel on the need for additional research funding.

Rhett tapped the paper with the back of his hand. Now, that's who he needed to get Pop in to see.

Before he could pull out his phone to make an appointment, his cell buzzed in his pocket. He fished it out and glanced at the caller's name. "Hey, Judith."

"Rhett, what time do you get in tomorrow? Stengel is clearly in over his head on this Markowitz deal. We need you back." She didn't wait for him to respond before going on. "I've set up a meeting at nine a.m. sharp. The big conference room."

Rhett's chest thudded painfully as he dropped into his father's warn leather chair. The earthy scent of weathered hide wafted up to him, reminding him of years gone by when he sat at the foot of this very chair while his dad powered through paperwork for the oyster farm. The smell—so familiar—solidified his determination.

He couldn't go home. Not right now. He needed to take care of Pop. What kind of son would just leave knowing his dad was suffering mental decline? He took a deep breath, did a mental calculation in his mind. "Look, Judith. I know I promised I'd be back, but something has come up."

"What do you mean?" Her voice turned icy. "We need you."

"I know, I know. And I'd be there. It's just—well, I'm facing a bit of a family emergency. It's my father. His health."

"I'm sorry to hear that," Judith said, making a weak attempt to sound empathetic to the situation. "Obviously, that puts the company in a bind." She paused. "Look, I don't want to be a hard nose here. But this Markowitz deal is critical. We simply can't afford for anything to go sideways. Delaying is not an option. I'm afraid if you can't make that meeting, I'll have to pull you off the account and let Phil step in."

Rhett's mind raced. Pull him? That was crazy!

"Judith, you can't do that." He launched into a campaign explaining why that would be a horrible decision when she cut him off.

"I'm sorry. There will be another deal," she told him. "When your family issues are resolved and you can make your responsibilities here a priority."

Ouch! There was no missing her message.

"Judith, wait—"

Click.

He pulled the phone from his ear and stared at the home screen. Did she really just hang up on him?

After everything he'd done for that company, she actually dismissed him because he couldn't make his work his priority? How many deals had he successfully shepherded to the closing table? More than he could count. His negotiation skills had made the firm a lot of money. That silver Jaguar Judith Sandidge drove? She custom-ordered that little baby in the aftermath of him single-handedly stealing the Barger deal away from a competitor. Everyone in his firm had benefited in some manner from his efforts. How dare she treat him like some simple employee who couldn't be counted on to close the deal? Especially when he'd proved otherwise. Anyone who knew him also knew this job had been his sole priority. She couldn't cut him a tiny bit of slack just this once?

Even as the thoughts stormed his mind, he knew if he was in Judith's shoes, he'd have made the same decision. He had in the past.

Just last year, Colin Treadwell fell into a deep clinical depression after losing his wife to cancer. Rhett sat opposite him and slid a generous check across the desk top. "Here's something to carry you until you're able to return to work. Go home, get well. And don't worry about your job. It'll be here waiting when you're ready to get back at it." Even as the words left his mouth, he knew, and likely so did Colin, that the firm waited for no one. There would be a replacement. High recruitment fees would be paid, if necessary, but they would replace him with only the very best candidate available. Sure, he'd be able to return at some point, but he'd walk back in the door with an invisible red X on his forehead—the mark that reminded everyone Colin had not powered through and brought his best to the work table.

In this very moment, Rhett wished he could go back and do right by Colin. Now, he understood. Still, Rhett wouldn't allow anyone, including Judith, to push him into a corner. When he had his dad properly evaluated and a plan in place, he'd return to work like a Boeing 707 skidding onto Main Street. He'd land back at the office and gain attention, make a splash. No recruit could recreate the relationships he'd built, employ the savvy he'd fostered. If Judith Sandidge was shortsighted and did not recognize him for the powerhouse he'd become, there were plenty of other financial firms across the country who would pay high six-figures as a sign-on bonus alone. He wasn't worried about it.

What Rhett was worried about right now was Pop.

He slid his finger across the face of his phone and dialed the number for Dr. Michaels. The effort took hours and just the right mixture of patience and determination, but he finally got through to the proper person and was able to make an appointment—an expedited one, at that.

No one could stop him when he put his mind to achieving a goal.

11

The following day began with a loud knock. "Rhett, dear," his mother called from behind the closed bedroom door. "Get up, son. We need to head out soon if we don't want to miss our scheduled launch."

"Yeah, okay. I'm up," he hollered back.

Rhett opened his eyelids, heavy from lack of sleep the night before. He reached and turned on the light on the bedside table, blinking several times to adjust to the brightness. Almost immediately, his conversation with Judith Sandidge entered his mind.

He was still plenty angry. He'd been mistreated, his contributions devalued. The least Judith could have done is to have extended a dab of support given everything he'd sacrificed for that company, for all the deals closed, money made. She hadn't. Instead, he was being replaced like a pair of worn loafers that had been shoved into the back of the closet in exchange for a new pair of Bruno Magli oxfords.

Rhett lifted the warm covers and sat up. Feeling instantly chilled, he grabbed a pair of jeans draped over the footboard and slid into them, then pulled on a flannel button-down. In the bathroom, he quickly brushed his teeth and ran a warm washcloth over his face. He wouldn't take time to shave. There was no need, really. Besides, he wasn't going to the office. A clean-shaven chin was of no consequence when on a fishing vessel.

Downstairs, in the kitchen, he greeted his mother with a quick kiss to the cheek.

"How'd you sleep, dear?" she asked, sliding a steaming travel mug of coffee into his hand.

"Great," he lied. He grabbed a warm, homemade maple bar from the plate on the counter. He swore his mom must never sleep.

Through the kitchen window, headlights reflected from where the lane turned off the highway. "Looks like your dad's back," she said, gazing out.

"Where's Jared?" he asked, wondering if Pop should even be driving alone until he was thoroughly evaluated and received a physician's okay.

"Your brother said he'd meet us there. Your sister, too. I think she was hoping Wes might remain home with the kids, but he wanted to fish."

Rhett gave her a distracted nod and took a sip of the hot coffee. One thing this family had learned, Wes never passed up food or fun.

The back door opened and in strode his dad. "Hey, Rhett. You ready to get your butt kicked? Been a while since you've held a rod and reel in your hands. Think you've forgotten how it's done?"

"Ha, that's doubtful, old man. You foolishly shared all your tricks with me years ago. I haven't forgotten. There's a mammoth-sized lingcod just waiting for me out there."

Pop's eyes sparkled, just like in the old days when Rhett was a kid and living at home. "You want to put some money on that?" he said, making a show of drawing his wallet from his jean's pocket.

Rhett's mom tossed a jacket at her husband. "Wylie, get your coat on. We've got to git."

Pop laughed and returned his wallet. "Fifty says the old man skunks you."

"You're on," Rhett said, following his folks out the door.

The marina was located nearly dead center in the middle of Pacific Bay. Bayfront ran along its wide u-shaped edge lined with restaurants, bars, and shops filled with souvenirs. While it remained too dark at this early hour to see clearly, Rhett could still make out a few windows with decorative shutters and some shops with striped canvas awnings. In the light from the lampposts, he could see pots lining the sidewalks filled with fall chrysanthemums and bright green potato vine flowing over the edges. All familiar sights. Pacific Bay was a quaint and pretty little tourist town. Fact was, he'd missed it.

Rhett pulled Pop's pickup to a stop and parked near the walkway that led to the bait shop where their family waited.

Leila's boys waved. "You're late," little Levi announced upon their approach. He pointed his dimpled finger at the new wristwatch Uncle Rhett had brought him all the way from Chicago.

"No, they're not late," argued Billy, pointing to his own watch. "The big hand is up at the twelve and the short hand is at the five. So, they are right on time." He looked to his uncle with an expectant smile. "Isn't that right, Uncle Rhett?"

Rhett deflated the argument by rubbing the top of both boys' heads. "The bigger question is, who wants a maple bar?" He nodded in the direction of his mother, who was carrying a clear plastic container covered by a pastel-colored lid.

"Me, me!" shouted Levi as he ran to his grandmother.

"Me, too!" called out Billy, scrambling after his brother. "I'll eat three of 'em."

Wes rubbed his open palms together. "Save some for me," he said.

Rhett's sister patted her husband's belly lovingly, then pulled a dog-eared romance novel from her bag. She held it up like a prize. "And people wonder why I read these," she said, laughing.

Allie appeared, standing at the edge of the boat where the boarding ramp connected to the deck. "Hey, y'all," she called out, waving. "Is the Duvall family ready to catch some fish?"

From what Rhett had heard, when Tarver McIntosh passed on, he left everything he owned, including this fishing boat, to his niece, prompting Allie to move to Pacific Bay from Texas, bringing her young son with her. Upon arrival, Allie discovered Tarver's house and boat left a lot to be desired. Rhett's mom reported the gal encountered many obstacles, including a boat fire, but eventually the tenacious young woman succeeded in rebuilding her uncle's business—a business that flourished today. Not only did Allie own the *Reel Chances*, but she'd been able to add two more vessels to her fishing fleet. She'd also married one of Rhett's best friends.

Rhett brushed a kiss to her cheek as he boarded. "So, you leave Cameron in bed this morning?"

She smiled. "Someone has to do the laundry and mop our kitchen floors. He drew the unlucky stick last night."

Rhett nodded slowly. "Ah, the fruit of marital bliss." He gave her a warm smile before following his sister inside the small cabin. Truth was, there were times he wondered what it would be like to be settled down, to know someone waited for him at home. Someone who was not only nice to look at, but intelligent and could engage in meaningful conversation that extended past the one-night-stand chatter he'd become accustomed to as of late.

Frankly, he'd been far too busy to invest in a relationship of that nature. His family often accused him of being married to his job. He supposed it was true. Turns out, she was a fickle mate.

As soon as they'd all donned life jackets and refilled their travel mugs with fresh brew from the coffee maker located in the tiny cabin, Allie gave the signal, and Captain Paul Hardy set the fishing vessel in motion. Minutes later, the boat chugged its way past the bay bridge and into open waters.

While most everyone remained in the cabin to ward off the brisk morning chill, Rhett joined his dad at the helm. Wylie gazed out over the open sea, holding his mug of steaming coffee. "Just never gets old."

"What's that, Pop?" Rhett asked, leaning slightly over the rail.

"This," he said. "The way the sea spray hits your face. The briny smell in the air. The way dawn hits the horizon with the thinnest of pale color before the sun pushes its way across the water."

Rhett faced him, tilted his head. "Pop, when did you gain a poet's way with words?"

For a moment, he saw the depths of certainty in his father's eyes. "No poet," Pop said. "I'm just a man who has learned what's important."

The two men didn't say anything more for several minutes. Finally, Rhett swallowed the lump building in his throat. "Pop, I'm sorry I haven't been here for you."

His dad patted his back. "You were busy, son. Besides, your brother has really stepped up, just like I told you. I may not be getting any younger, but there's still a good many years left for this set of skin and bones."

That brought a wistful smile to Rhett's face. His dad had always prided himself on working hard. Yet, he'd also taught his family how to have a good time, especially his boys. "Pop, do you remember that time we all went fishing to celebrate paying off the original expansion? I think I was, what, maybe twelve?"

His father nodded. "Jared was nine or so. All he did was follow you around the boat."

Rhett rubbed his stubbled chin. "Bugged the ever-loving crap out of me. I couldn't even bait the hook without him nosing in, wanting to see what I was doing."

"You two fought like crazy when you were young." His pop shook his head. "Never did quite understand it."

"That's because you never saw what I saw," Rhett explained. "Especially when he got older."

Wylie took a sip from his mug, wiped at the moisture that clung to his gray mustache. "Jared had his own ways."

Rhett stared at the horizon, now the shade of orange sherbet, the kind he used to love as a kid. He would like to beat his point home, remind his dad of all the times Jared had failed to live up to the standards Pop had set for his family. Surely, Pop hadn't forgotten the late-night calls from Willard Peters down at the sheriff's office. Did Rhett need to remind him of the occasion where his youngest son had toilet-papered the large lodgepole pine in the churchyard? Pop didn't even ground him for that antic. Yet, Rhett clearly recalled getting a speeding ticket—the only one in his entire life—and Pop coming down hard on him, lecturing how his carelessness could have hurt someone. Driving was a privilege. A privilege that would be revoked if he didn't slow down.

Despite the inequity, Pop had also been good to him. Rhett recalled how badly he'd wanted to raise a calf and enter it in the county fair, just like his buddies Ben and Cam. At dinner that night, his mother quickly reminded them all how little spare time Rhett had after school and chores, that neither she nor his father would step in and take over when he tired of the project.

Rarely did Pop ever go against Mom in matters, especially those concerning the children. He believed in a united front. This time, Pop scraped the last of the meatloaf from his plate and thought a minute before responding. When he did, he surprised them all by saying he supported the idea.

"Like your mother indicated, this will be your responsibility, Rhett. And yours alone. No one else in the family will feed or care for the animal."

Rhett could hardly contain his excitement. "I will—I mean, you can count on me, Mom. I won't back off my responsibilities, Pop. You both can rely on me to follow through and not disappoint you."

Even though the family budget was tighter back then, his dad took him to the auction and bid on a little black-and-white heifer. Over the course of months, Rhett was true to his word. He faithfully rose from his bed every morning and went out to the pen Pop built behind his mother's gardening shed and filled the trough with hay and the bucket with water. He walked the heifer every evening after dinner, training her on the lead rope.

When it came time to load up his heifer and head to the fair, Pop surprised him again with permission to spend the night in the fair barn, all by himself. Well, alone except for all the other kids hanging out with their animals before the big day in the show ring.

"Oh, Wylie. Are you sure?" his mother had questioned. "Is he old enough?"

Pop placed his hand on her shoulder. "Age is just a number. What matters is his level of maturity." Pop turned, looked him directly in the eyes. "You understand what I'm saying, son?"

Rhett nodded with enthusiasm. "Yes, sir. I won't do anything you wouldn't approve of."

It was only about a half-hour past midnight when the situation went south. His heifer became agitated, had labored breathing. Rhett became instantly worried, especially when he noticed bloody diarrhea in the straw.

Panicked, Rhett ran to a phone and called his dad, woke him up. "Pop, she's sick. Maybell is sick!"

His dad arrived within the hour. After confirming the animal was indeed ill, he called Dr. Art Pierard, the town vet. It didn't take long for Dr. Pierard to come up with a diagnosis—prussic acid poisoning. While rare, some animals succumbed after eating native sudangrass.

Unfortunately, his heifer was dead by morning.

"There wasn't anything anyone could have done, son," Pop told him on the way home, in an attempt to console him. Rhett tried his hardest not to cry. He was far too old for that. Even so, his vision blurred with moisture.

"It's not fair," he claimed. "Why did my heifer have to get sick? I did everything I was asked. I took good care of her."

His wise father stared at the road through the windshield of his old truck. "Sometimes, boy, you can do everything right, and still events don't go as we hope. These things are often out of our hands."

Rhett gripped the boat railing and gazed out over the water, filling with affection for the man beside him. He tried to imagine his father changed, imagined what it would be like if the things he'd read about on the internet these past days actually came to pass. How long before Pop's decline raced forward, robbing him of precious memory. Would his dad reach a point where he wouldn't be able to hand out that sage advice he was known for?

Rhett's determination became as hard and unbending as the metal railing.

Not on his watch.

While he hadn't intended to bring the subject up now, it seemed the perfect time. "Pop, I've made an appointment for you in Portland. I want you to be evaluated by Dr. Michaels. He's the best."

"Evaluated?"

"Pop, your memory. You—"

His dad huffed. "Look, I don't know what you think you

know, but it's not as bad as you think. I don't want your mother getting upset. Understand?"

"But, Pop. I think—"

His dad scowled and tossed his remaining coffee over the rail. "You heard me."

Suddenly, the boat engine slowed, signaling Captain Hardy had found a school of fish on his sonar equipment.

The door to the cabin flung open, and out poured his nephews. They ran forward. "Boys, slow down," Leila called out after them. "You were told. You need to stay close to me."

Wes shoved the remaining bite of a maple bar into his mouth. "Don't run," he warned, with his mouth full.

While the deckhand passed out baited rods to everyone, Allie moved to the handheld microphone, broadcasting her voice. "So, you all know the drill. When you get a bite, yell, 'fish on!' That will signal Captain Paul to cut the engine so we can get the nets and haul in your catch."

Everyone nodded that they understood. Wylie and Grace moved to the starboard side and stood a few feet from each other. They cast out before Pop's arm found its way around his wife's shoulders, pulling her close for warmth. Wes, Leila and the boys were at the rear of the boat. Rhett positioned himself on the port side of the vessel. Jared joined him.

"So, what were you and Pop in such deep discussion about?" Jared asked, not even waiting until he had his line in the water.

The boat gently rose and fell with the swells. Rhett clicked his reel and drew his line taut. "Not sure I know what you mean?"

Jared swung his rod over the water, watched as the bait made a splash on the surface. "You and Pop. You were talking."

Rhett grew immediately aggravated. He wanted to tell his little brother to butt out. He was not obligated to share every discussion he had with his parents, and especially anything he talked over with Pop. Still, there was a fine line between being assertive and being a jerk. "You must have a reason for asking," he answered, diverting from a real response. He paused, scanned the horizon. "Look, okay...allow me to just put the cards on the table here. I told Pop I'd made an appointment for him to see Dr. Michaels at the Brain Institute at OHSU in Portland."

There, his intentions were out in the open. Jared would have no choice but to deal with it.

"I see."

Rhett steeled himself against what he knew was coming. Several seconds passed before Jared finally added, "Look, I know you love Pop. We all do. But aren't you moving a little too fast on all this?"

Rhett breathed in slowly, surprised Jared had not erupted in anger. Taking the opening, he explained everything he'd read, the risks of waiting to properly diagnose and treat what he strongly suspected his dad was dealing with. "I know you and Mom may not agree with what I've done, but I'm asking you to trust me on this."

A look of resignation crossed his brother's face. They both knew there was little to no opportunity to change Rhett's mind and the course he'd set out. "All I ask is that you stop and consider their wishes," Jared told him. "It really is Mom and Dad's decision how to proceed."

"I know that," Rhett argued. "We both know denial can be at play, and sticking heads in the sand is not doing Pop any good. Once we know what we're dealing with, we can develop a plan and execute it. We'll all know what to expect. The unknown is always much scarier." He paused, then decided to make his position absolutely clear. "I made an appointment, and I'm taking Pop to Portland."

Jared's pole suddenly dipped, signaling he had a bite. "Fish on," he called out.

The engine cut, and the boat drifted to a stop as Jared reeled in his catch. Levi and Billy ran to join them. As Jared pulled in a nice-sized red snapper, the two younger boys both jumped up and down with excitement.

Billy scrambled for the wooden club, held out an open arm to keep his younger brother from getting any closer. "Stand back. I'll do it," he claimed, as his uncle placed the flopping fish inside the basket.

Levi's face fell with disappointment. "That's not fair! Who made you the boss of everything?"

Billy grabbed the club, raised it in the air. "Because I'm the oldest, and I know how better than you. That's why."

Then, he bent and whacked the fish on the head.

12

That evening, after dinner, Rhett realized he'd had enough family time for a while. He needed to get away and be alone, to think and get his head on straight. The tension was getting to him. He highly suspected Jared had cornered their mom and tattled on him, enlightened her to Rhett's plans. The signs were subtle but clearly there. It seemed she might be avoiding him and never looking him in the eye.

"I'll be out for a while tonight. Don't wait up," he told her at the sink. He leaned in and brushed a quick kiss against her soft cheek. She didn't answer. Instead, she simply brushed the hair away from her face with her forearm and nodded.

Upstairs, he slipped into his favorite pair of Air Jordans and pulled on a worn hoodie. He grabbed his cell, tucked it in his jean's pocket, and headed for the stairs. In his rental, he turned on the radio, hoping to lose himself in his favorite local station broadcast out of Salem, a station that played hits from his high school years non-stop after closing out the six o'clock news.

High school seemed like a long time ago. A time when

things were much simpler. A time when he didn't feel pulled between his career and family obligations. A time when he wasn't letting people down and seen as the enemy simply because he wanted what was best for his dad.

After driving a short distance past the center of town, Rhett turned from the main highway onto a narrow, winding road that led to a secluded area of the beach and parked. He pulled the strings on his hoodie to tighten the fabric around his neck as protection against the evening chill before he cut the engine. A run would do him some good.

"Man, just look at that," he muttered as he stepped from the truck, appreciating the view that never got old. While he loved running along Lakefront Trail in Chicago, the waterfront views couldn't begin to compare to Oregon's coastline and its rugged rock outcroppings, the Pacific Bay Bridge spanning the inlet and the lighthouse out on the point jutting into the sky, a beacon of familiarity.

Rhett loved Pacific Bay at this hour, right before the sky started to darken and when ocean breezes grew still and the water's surface calmed, especially at low tide—when waves edged with foam crept onshore and slowly retreated in rhythm, leaving unbroken sand dollars littering the hard-packed sand.

His favorite running spot was a stretch of beach that ran north from the lighthouse along a rocky coastline lined with homes offering million-dollar views. In the distance, he could see the Bayfront Restaurant, a favorite eating establishment perched on a cliff located at the end of a promontory overlooking the ocean.

For a brief moment, he was jealous of his buddies who lived in Pacific Bay, the ones who graduated and had stayed, embracing the familiar and who had continued making the tiny coastal town their home.

Rhett loved the city, the bustle and towering office buildings, the museums, the parties and nightlife, baseball and the great hot dogs. He loved it all. Certainly, he'd accomplished amazing things in his profession, but moving to Chicago had definitely been a tradeoff. In the short time he'd been home, he was beginning to realize the distance he felt from this place and from his family and friends could not simply be measured in miles.

Rhett squared his shoulders and set out, jogging down an incline lined with sea grass until his feet hit the wide spans of wet sand. From the look of things, the tides were just now beginning to change.

GRACE SAT on the edge of the quilted bed, watching Wylie unbuttoning his shirt. "What's the matter, Wyatt? You look troubled."

Wylie tossed his shirt over the back of the rocking chair. "Rhett knows," he told her, running his hand over his balding head.

Grace drew a deep breath, hating the expression she saw on her husband's face. "We knew it was only a matter of time, sweetheart." She reached for her brush, then ran it through her cropped curls.

"Here, let me." Wylie stepped close, took the brush from her hand and used it to stroke her hair. "He's made me an appointment to see a specialist—in Portland."

Grace closed her eyes, not entirely surprised at the news but wishing their oldest son would just let things be. "When?"

Wylie leaned and kissed the top of his wife's head. "Later this week."

Grace turned. "Did you tell him we'd already talked to doctors?"

He nodded. "Of course. Rhett wasn't going to be satisfied with that. You know our boy."

Tears welled. "Yes, I know our boy. Why can't he just back off for once, let us protect him from—well, from all this. Specialists disagree on so much and if you go looking, you can always find someone willing to sing doom and gloom." She rubbed at her forehead. "He'll somehow take all this on as his own, you know."

Wylie slowly nodded. "Yup. He's wired that way."

"Rhett's going to believe the worst. He'll have you completely demented and sitting in a chair staring at the wall." She grabbed her husband's work-calloused hand. "We don't know what is ahead exactly, but Wylie—we both agreed, right? We're not going to borrow trouble. You heard what Dr. Cannon said. We all get forgetful as we age."

Wylie looked at her with that understanding only he had. His fingers stroked her hair. "Ah, that's what I love about you, darlin'. In a pile of dung, you always look for the pony."

They both knew Wylie's more realistic assessment would likely be more accurate. Dr. Cannon had warned that Alzheimer's disease was progressive. If Wylie's case was confirmed, his cognitive state would eventually decline. They'd agreed the key was not to give in to a grim prognosis.

In light of that, they'd decided not to go forward with further testing. "Let's just let this play out, Wylie. Please?" she'd begged. "Take the medications, but I don't want to know the worst-case scenario. All that will do is rob of our hope, our joy."

He loved her and had consented to her wishes.

Thankfully, both Jared and Leila had not pressed the issue. There was an unspoken agreement to pause, an agreement to allow them all to adjust until circumstances no longer allowed them to simply live in the moment.

Now, Rhett was home and aware. Unlike his siblings, he would never let this go, no matter their desire or wishes to take things slow. Free-falling simply wasn't in their oldest son's nature.

Grace turned and took her husband's chin in her fingers. She searched his eyes before letting her hands drop back into her lap. "You gave in."

He slowly nodded, took her hands in his own. "It will be all right, sweetheart. No matter what. We're in this together, and I'll never let you go."

She laid her head against his shoulder, wanting beyond anything to believe what he said was true. Yet, deep inside, she had to acknowledge that her dear Wylie may not have a say in the situation. If he indeed had Alzheimer's, no amount of steel resolve would matter. He would leave her...eventually.

RHETT FINISHED A QUARTER-MILE SPRINT, no longer jogging but running at full speed. He slowed to a stop and bent over to catch his breath. Salty air stung his lungs as his chest heaved. When his breaths became more normal, he lifted again.

Down the beach, in the distance, a woman with long blonde hair threw a stick for a large black-and-white dog. She waited for the long-legged canine to chase and bring it back, then bent and retrieved the stick and repeated the process. She wore jeans and a red rain slicker. He walked her way and gave a little wave in her direction. That's when he realized the woman was Diane Jeffers. What was her married name again? He couldn't remember.

"Hey, Rhett," she called out, waving back.

He jogged up to her. "Great dog."

Diane let out a laugh. "Well, I don't know about how great he is, but he's loved."

Rhett bent to pet the dog's head. "What breed?"

"Mutt—pure mutt." She clipped a leash on his collar. "His name is Dill, as in pickle. My daughter named him."

Rhett's eyebrows lifted. "Unusual, but I like it." He let his gaze meet hers. "She sounds like she has a sense of humor," he offered. "Your daughter."

"Well, maybe," Diane admitted. "More like she refuses to live within any boundaries."

"Not a bad thing," Rhett suggested.

"So, you going for a run?" She flushed a little. "That's obvious, I suppose. What I mean is, do you come out often? Thanks to Dill's need to expend unending energy, I'm here on the beach frequently, and I haven't seen you on this stretch before."

Rhett walked alongside her. "Yeah, I'm a runner. Unfortunately, I haven't found the time to jog the beach since arriving. Tonight, I just needed to clear my head a bit. Nothing like running on packed sand and listening to surf to help square up your mind."

Diane's eyes filled with laughter. "Ah, yes. I know that one. Needing to square up, I mean."

He found her honesty refreshing. Most people he knew had a hard time admitting any level of struggle. He certainly wasn't accustomed to letting on that he didn't have it all together.

"Hey, you up for a drink?" Rhett pointed to the lights from Bayfront Restaurant up on the cliff above.

She stared at him for a few seconds, shrugged. "Well, I'd have to drop the dog off at my mom's. She doesn't live far." Her face broke into a slight smile. "Sure, why not. Instead, I'm going to extend that invitation to dinner. I haven't eaten yet, and I'm starving."

"Sounds great!" He'd already eaten, but he was up for a bowl of clam chowder. "Now, you're not going to go and change or anything. Right? Because, well—I'm in my running clothes."

She quickly shook her head. "Nope. These days, what you see is what you get with me."

He smiled at that. All the more reason to like her.

They parted, promising to meet each other at the restaurant in twenty minutes. Rhett wasn't sure why he hadn't gotten to know Diane more when they were in high school. What he remembered about her was that she was really nice but kept to herself, for the most part. In fact, he'd had a bit of a crush on her. Right after school, she was gone. At the time, no one really knew where she'd moved. She was smart, so he'd figured she took off for college somewhere.

He heard she rarely made visits home. Last year, he was surprised to see her on television and learned her husband was making a senatorial run and had fallen into a scandal by having an affair with someone from his staff. Cam and Ben said she'd moved back home in the aftermath. He also learned she had a daughter and that Craig Anthony was the father. Obviously, there was a story there. Unlike his buddies, he wasn't one to dig into other people's business. He had enough to worry about without scooping other people's troubles onto his plate.

The Bayfront Restaurant had long been one of his favorites in Pacific Bay. Few places could boast casual dining in such an elegant setting. Well, elegant for a tiny coastal town. What made the place so spectacular were the panoramic views of the ocean. The establishment was known for tiny tables tucked in around large glass windows overlooking the surf below and providing magazine-quality images of the sunset. The food was superb and featured the catch of the day—fresh fish brought in off the boats daily. The clam chowder was served in large ceramic bowls and was thick as gravy, served with a full pat of butter melting on top. The staff was friendly and the drinks generous. His kind of place.

"Hey, Henson!" Rhett said, greeting the proprietor as he entered the restaurant.

"Well, Rhett Duvall. It's been a while," he said, shaking Rhett's extended hand, then leaning in for a hug and patting him on the back with gusto. "How long you back in town for? Sorry I couldn't make your dad's party. This place, well—she's like a woman about to give birth, always requires my full attention." Henson looked him over. "You never change. Look like the same kid who ran that football down the field." He glanced over Rhett's shoulder. "You alone?"

"I'm meeting someone. Diane Jeffers."

The old man nodded. "Ah, yes. Another sheep returned home to the fold. Can't say as I blame anyone for finding their way back to Pacific Bay, no matter what the reason. Home is where the heart is—and few leave the place and take their heart with them."

Rhett was beginning to agree to some degree.

"Let's seat you and Diane over here." Henson pointed to a little table located in a private cove. Like the rest, the table had a flickering candle centered on top of a white linen tablecloth.

"The table's great. Thanks." It dawned on him Henson may have misunderstood and thought he had Diane were on a date. "I ran into Diane down on the beach and asked her to join me for a drink. Just to catch up. We're old friends," he clarified, knowing how rumors got started in this town. He'd be leaving eventually, but Diane had to live here and wrestle the gossip mill.

Henson's bushy brows rose slightly. "Of course." With a twinkle in his watery blue eyes, he winked and left Rhett standing by the table.

When seated, Rhett pulled out his phone and glanced at the screen. No messages. No calls. No texts.

He sighed and slid it back in his pocket, holding back the strange feeling. He'd never before felt like he was dangling at the end of a rope no one was holding. A secret part of him wished that Phil Stengel would botch everything, that Judith would call and admit she'd been hasty in pulling Rhett from the Markowitz deal. He checked his phone regularly, just in case. He imagined just how the conversation would go.

"You were right," Judith would have to admit. "We need you. I've been forced to reconsider. Please return to the account. We'll work with you. Zoom calls, if necessary. Just come back and help bring this one in."

He'd be gracious, of course. Act like the consummate professional he was known to be. Still, there would be markers he'd call on later. Returned favors as a payback for his willingness to move past the way Judith had so quickly dismissed him. Maybe a director title.

So far, no contact.

He pulled the phone out again, slipped onto the internet, and checked the Dow.

"Hey," Diane's voice pulled him from the phone. "I hope I didn't keep you waiting too long."

He abandoned his phone and looked up. She'd brushed her hair back into a ponytail and had put some color on her lips. He was unsure why, exactly, but the thought lifted his spirits.

"Hey," he said, wishing he'd made a quick trip to the restroom and cleaned up a bit as well, at least ran a wet paper towel over his face to clean off the dried sweat.

He stood and pulled out her chair. She slid into it and thanked him. "It's been a while since I've been here," she admitted, taking in the place. "I'd forgotten how much I love it."

"Me too. Can I get you something to drink?" He motioned for the waitress, who hurried over to take their order.

"I'll have a bourbon, straight up." He looked across the table at her. "I hear the rum mojitos are good here."

She shook her head. "I don't drink anymore."

"Oh." Her answer gave him pause. "Well, something else?"

She smiled at the waitress. "I'll have a coconut spritzer, with a twist of lime." When the waitress left the table, she turned to him. "I suppose you heard I had a time of it last year. My choices, bad choices actually, well—they caught up with me. I got to the end of that wild journey and discovered I had a drinking problem. Thanks to my mom and daughter's intervention, I saw the light. I subjected myself to a brief rehab stay, and I attend AA meetings regularly. So far, I've stayed sober. A fact I'm very proud of."

He immediately grew concerned. "I'm sorry. I can change my order—"

"No, no—it's okay. I can be around alcohol. In fact, it's part of my journey to health—learning to not avoid circumstances, but move through them without tumbling into an emotional abyss." She must've seen the relief on his face because she immediately added. "I'm good. Really."

Rhett quickly considered this. How the woman across the table from him had struggled with addiction and had beat the beast. He admired that.

Just as quickly, a thought formed. Jared had done the same—or so he claimed. Why couldn't he extend a similar level of admiration toward his brother's effort? He brushed the thought from his mind, focused on Diane. "You have a right to be proud of moving forward like you have."

She fingered the folded linen napkin on the table before her. "Well, it's nothing you do alone."

Another thought formed. Hadn't his mother claimed Jared attended the AA meetings as well? Did Jared and Diane know each other—perhaps confided their struggles, and the cause, in those meetings? While he'd never attended Alcoholics Anonymous meetings himself, he'd seen them enough on television and knew the way attendees seemed to dump their darkest secrets—confidentially, of course. In fact, wasn't the fact you were even there kept confidential? Diane wouldn't likely tell him if Jared attended the meetings with her, even if he asked. So, he didn't. Instead, he changed the subject. "I don't need to look at the menu to know I'm going to order a bowl of Henson's clam chowder."

Diane's lips drew up in a tiny grin. She, no doubt, recognized his tactic and went along. "Not me. I'm in the mood for some fish."

The waitress appeared with their drinks. She took the menus she'd folded under her arms and placed them on the table.

As promised, Rhett didn't bother to open his. "I'll have a bowl of the clam chowder."

"Bread with that?" the waitress asked.

"You bet."

She looked to Diane. "Do you have any questions?" Then, leaning forward, she confided, "I highly recommend the grouper, freshly caught this morning down off Fisherman's Point. It's poached, then flash sauteed with garlic, white wine, capers and wild mushrooms."

Diane lifted her brows. "Wow. That sounds delicious. Sign me up."

Rhett reached for his bourbon. He took a sip, then moved the glass in a slow circular motion to run the bourbon through the chipped ice. "So, it's been a while."

"Yes," she agreed. "We definitely need to catch up." She took a sip of her spritzer. "You first."

He smiled at her. "What do you want to know?"

"Everything," she urged. "Tell me everything."

"Well, I've been living in the Midwest," he told her. "I worked for a private equity fund in Chicago."

"Past tense?" she asked.

"Huh?" Only then did he realize what he'd said. "Oh, no. I—I'm still there. Uh, just on a sabbatical." He spilled about his concern for his dad, something he rarely did. It wasn't his style to spread his family business around. "We have an appointment at the Brain Institute at Oregon Health Sciences University. From what I've read, the team is one of the best in the country when it comes to frontotemporal dementia and related disorders."

"I'm so sorry," she said. "I had no idea."

"Yeah, we're not making the news widely known," he told her. "As you can imagine, Pop would have my hide if he thought I was discussing his medical issue with anyone."

She shrugged. "Smart of him. People like to talk."

Rhett nodded. "Yeah, they sure do."

She looked at his hand as he lifted his glass to his lips a second time. "No ring. You're not married?"

Rhett shook his head. "I got engaged once. She broke it off when she discovered how little time I had to invest in a relationship." He gave a nervous laugh before admitting, "Ha, didn't even have time for a dog." He took a long draw off his bourbon. "One of several terminated relationships."

Surprisingly, his comment made her laugh. "You talk about the women in your life like they were business deals."

He laughed too. "Well, now you know why the women in my life always came to their senses and moved on." Rhett found himself feeling self-conscious. In most situations, he'd divert the conversation to his career accomplishments, carefully detail how he'd begun working fresh after graduating college as an entry-level financial analyst. He'd enrolled in Loyola and obtained a master's in finance while doing double duty climbing the corporate ladder. He'd toss out his impressive resume, reciting his accolades and progression into senior-level positions. At cocktail parties, he'd often regale his audience with anecdotes of how he'd pulled one deal after another out of the toilet and modestly let it slip how much money he'd made the firm.

Somehow, he instinctively knew none of that would impress the woman sitting across from him. If the stories he'd read were true, she'd lived in that world. Money would not have its normal compulsory glitter effect. Nor would the fact he'd finally been able to purchase his coveted Audi R8 Spyder and pay cash.

Rhett couldn't cling to any of his typical crutches, and it surprised him how freeing that felt.

The waitress reappeared at the table with their food. Rhett placed the napkin across his lap and scooped a big bite of soup into his spoon, held it in the air. "How about you?" he asked before taking the bite.

Diane spread her napkin across her lap as well. "I can't believe there's much I can tell you that you haven't seen in the news," she said, lifting her fork.

"I only follow financial news," he answered. "So try me." One day she was gone. He hadn't known what happened, but he'd sure missed seeing her in the halls and around town after school.

"Well, wow. Where do I start?"

"How about at the beginning?" he urged, before taking another bite.

Over the next minutes, she confided that she'd had a little-known relationship with Craig Anthony and found herself pregnant. "I felt so foolish," she admitted. "And scared. There were options presented to me. Some good, some bad. In the end, I elected to take off and quietly leave town before anyone found out. In large part, I wanted to protect my mom from the disgrace. Society at large may have socially progressed. That said, Pacific Bay was, and perhaps still is, cemented in a sense of morality that doesn't include sleeping around without being married. At least not out in the open. Especially not back then."

"Oh, I'm not sure that's true," Rhett argued. "Those morals didn't seem to stifle the activities of the guys I hung with in high school."

"It was different for the female gender," she reminded. "At the very least, I knew my mom would have a fit. Frankly, I wasn't up for the judgment I knew I'd suffer—from her, and everyone else."

Rhett's heart sank to hear that. True, small towns could be brutal in their attitudes of self-righteous indignation when someone fell from grace. He also knew the extent of compassion the town often portrayed, especially to one of their own. Yes, they'd have been shocked. There would have been whispered chatter about the matter for a number of months. In the end, gossip would have quieted, and Diane and her child would have been folded into the community—remaining a treasured part of the fabric of the town. Hadn't they done just that for his brother? He was sad to learn she'd chosen to run.

"What did you do then?" he asked.

Her eyes crinkled in laughter as she began. "Well, I climbed on the merry-go-round called marriage, moving from one shiny painted horse to another, until finally the music quit playing and I was forced to climb down and walk on my own two feet."

"Come again?"

"Husband number one was Garrison O'Keefe. He owned a conglomerate of movie theaters. I really loved him, or so I thought. Sadly, he turned out to be gay. Left me for a guy named Kevin."

She scooped a piece of fish onto her fork. "Husband number two was Andrew Michels. He swept Stacey and me off to Maui, where we lived for a little over a year until he found a younger island girl and dumped me." She took the bite of fish and chewed while continuing to talk. "Jay Hawkins was my third husband. He was a spoiled rich kid from Pasadena who inherited his daddy's commercial real estate business. He paid for these." She pointed to her chest. "And paid for hip liposuction before moving on to a young starlet who appeared on *The Bachelorette*. He not only gave that blonde tart a rose, but endowed her with her own float in the Rose Bowl Parade the following year."

She saw him staring at her chest and grinned. "What? You think I suddenly grew boobs after I graduated?"

Embarrassed that she caught him looking, he pulled his attention to his empty glass of bourbon and motioned for the waitress to bring him another.

"And, finally—husband number four. The real gem of them all. I met Richard Park while attending a party for volunteers put on by his campaign office. That's when he ran for Laguna Beach city council. He won, of course. I was terribly impressed."

Diane took another bite and grinned over at him. "There you have it. Diane Jeffers's husband parade."

"Did you love them?"

"Oh, yes," she admitted. "All of them. Or, at least I thought I did."

Curiosity got the better of him. "And now? Is Craig Anthony—?"

"Oh, goodness no!" she quickly said. "Craig is Stacey's real father. A fact he only learned once I moved back. We're friendly, but not really friends. Too much baggage, I suppose."

Rhett nodded, surprised at the relief he felt at her confession that she and Craig were not in any kind of relationship. "So, what now?"

"Now, I simply enjoy my daughter. I'm forming a renewed relationship with my mother. We're becoming friends—something I never thought I'd be able to say. I'm learning to live in the moment, not in the past and not in the future. I try to stay present and I've made a commitment to wring every sweet drop of joy out of this gift we call life."

He noticed, then, that tears had formed. "Diane, you're crying."

"Yeah, I suppose I am," she said, in that calm, lovely voice. She wiped at her eyes. "Can't help it. I get a bit emotional when I think of where I was—and where I now am."

On instinct, Rhett reached across the table for her hand and gave it a squeeze. "I wished we'd known each other better back then. Maybe I could have been there for you. Regardless, I'm glad we've reconnected," he told her. He meant it. Somehow, he knew he'd found a friend.

Given what was likely ahead with his dad, his family, his job—well, he was going to need one.

13

The morning of Wylie's doctor appointment dawned with an overcast sky. Clouds hung low over the bay and spat at Rhett and his folks with occasional droplets through a light fog as they made their way out to the rental car.

"I still don't know why we have to make a trip all the way to Portland when we've already seen a doctor," Grace said over her shoulder. She shook her head and tucked herself into the back seat.

"Mom, we've been over this," Rhett reminded as he closed the door behind her. He climbed into the driver's seat and turned on the ignition as Wylie entered the car from the opposite side. "Dr. Michaels is a specialist. He's led a team of highly respected researchers at the Brain Institute. He's considered the best of the best."

"I'm not sure he can add to what we already know," his mother muttered.

The drive to Portland took a little over two hours. Rhett drove his folks and Jared and Leila followed in Jared's pickup.

Wes had stayed home with the boys, his cooperation secured by Rhett's offer to pay for pizza delivery and a six-pack.

The parking lot was full, which caused Rhett to have to circle around hunting for a spot, even at this early hour. He found himself getting insanely aggravated on the third pass, especially when his mother kept pointing. "There, son. There's one." Then she'd sigh, "Oh, never mind. It's taken."

Finally, he spotted a van with its rear lights on, indicating an intention to back up. Rhett's jaw stiffened as he pulled to a stop and waited, giving the guy plenty of room to back up. Seconds later, there was no movement. Rhett laid on the horn.

"Honey, have some patience," his mother quickly admonished.

It took everything in Rhett to remain quiet. Finally, the slow-poke pulled from the spot and Rhett was able to ease his rental car in place.

The Oregon Health Sciences University lobby was buzzing with activity. A long granite counter was located at the back of the large area. The wall behind the counter was decorated with stone and a calming waterfall fell into a water feature.

Several patients and their families lined up in front of the counter, waiting for directions and instructions on how to check in for their appointments. Rhett tucked his jacket over his arm and led his folks across the shiny floor to their place in line.

"How long do you think this will take?" his mother asked, her voice filled with apprehension.

"How long what will take?" Wylie asked, his expression confused.

Rhett scowled. "Your appointment, Pop. Remember? We're here to see Dr. Michaels?"

His dad lifted his chin. "I remember."

Rhett wasn't so sure he had remembered. Twice this morning, he'd had to mention the appointment to his dad. Once, when he'd pulled on his mucking boots and headed across the lawn to the oyster beds like it was a normal workday.

Now that Rhett was aware his dad was struggling, he saw a lot of evidence. He forgot to tie his shoe and nearly tripped over the string in the kitchen. His pop paused on the way down the hallway, unsure which door led to the bathroom. Rhett opened the refrigerator door to find Pop's reading glasses on the shelf next to the carton of milk. He left the front door open on numerous occasions. All minor, but growing evidence that Rhett had made the right decision making this appointment and forcing the issue.

The lady behind the counter called them forward just as Rhett spotted Jared and Leila sitting in the waiting area. How had Jared beaten them in?

His mother took a look at his expression and leaned over to his ear. "He must've found a spot before we did."

Rhett slid his folder across the desk to the woman. Inside were all the important insurance papers she'd need. He'd done all he could online beforehand, but some things would only be accomplished with proper identification and such.

Minutes later, they were all set. He led his folks over and sat with them near where Jared and Leila were waiting.

"Not sure why Jared had to take the day off for this. I don't like leaving the operation with no one there," his dad said, leaning over with his elbows on his knees.

"Everything's fine, Pop," Jared assured. "Alfredo is in charge."

Alfredo Munoz had been their line supervisor for over a decade. He was capable, dependable—qualities Rhett knew his dad respected.

Wylie nodded his approval.

Grace took out her bag and pulled some knitting needles and yarn. She jabbed the needles together, casting on several stitches. "I still believe the diagnosis from Dr. Cannon in

Astoria was just fine. We really didn't need to all traipse all the way to Portland to hear what we already know."

This time Leila spoke up. "It can't hurt, Mom."

Rhett gave his sister an appreciative nod.

Jared folded his arms across his chest. "Yeah, can't hurt. Besides, it'll make Rhett feel better."

"What do you mean by that?" Rhett demanded. "What do you mean it'll make *me* feel better? It should make all of us feel better. Dr. Michaels is the most respected expert in this field. He'll be able to assess Pop and assure all of us we're doing all we can to make sure—"

His mother's eyes narrowed. "You've told us, Rhett. We're here. Let's just get all this behind us."

The sharp reprimand from his mother gut-punched him. Yes, he knew she was against further evaluation. Over and over, she'd made her position on the matter clear. She was likely scared to find out what was ahead. If she'd looked on the internet like he had, the information could be grim. For that reason, he forced himself to let the hurt go. She was afraid, that's all.

Pop stood. "Jared, you might want to go on home. Who's going to take care of things on the line today? We need you there."

Jared rubbed at his chin. "Alfredo will take care of everything, Pop."

Wylie's eyebrows pulled together in concern. "Alfredo?"

Jared patiently nodded and motioned for their dad to sit back down. "Alfredo's got it covered."

Their mother crammed her knitting needles inside her bag. "What time is our appointment?"

"Ten o'clock," Rhett reported. "But they warned they were running a bit late."

As if on cue, a woman wearing slacks and a white medical jacket appeared. "Mr. Duvall?"

Grace and Wylie stood in unison. "This is Mr. Duvall," Grace said, motioning to her husband.

The woman gave them a warm smile. "I'm Jacqueline Reynolds, Dr. Michaels's nurse practitioner. Let's have you all follow me."

Dr. Michaels's office was on the fourth floor. Ms. Reynolds got them all seated in around a small conference table to the right of his desk. A credenza held a framed photo of what appeared to be his family—he was flanked by a wife with long blonde hair and two well-dressed children. The walls were decorated with framed licenses and awards, a few displaying articles from prestigious medical publications.

They waited only minutes before the door opened, and Dr. Michaels walked in. He greeted them with a wide smile, then held out his arm to Wylie. "Well, it's nice to finally meet you, Mr. Duvall. May I call you Wylie?"

Rhett's pop nodded. "It's nice to meet you as well."

"Yes," Rhett's mom added. "We appreciate you taking the time to see Wylie."

Dr. Michaels slid into a place on the nearby sofa. He held up a folder packed with papers. "I've reviewed Wylie's medical history, including all of Dr. Cannon's records." He looked directly at Grace. "He's a fine physician, a colleague I greatly admire."

That was a nice touch, Rhett thought. One that seemed to instantly put his mother more at ease.

"This is only a start, but I'd like to ask you some questions, Wylie. Would that be all right?"

Wylie nodded. "Sure, let's get this over with. I have a lot of work to do back home and need to get to it."

Dr. Michaels smiled. "We'll hasten things up and get you back on the road as soon as possible. So, shall we get started?" He pulled his desk chair from around his desk and positioned it in front of Wylie, bringing with him a pad of lined paper and a pen.

Rhett listened intently as Dr. Michaels started with a battery of questions. Did he know what day of the week it was? He asked whether he was having any difficulty sleeping and tested him on his memory of a number of life details—his family's names and birth dates, facts about the town and state he lived in, when he was married and where. Pop passed most of these with only a little hesitation.

Then came a series of questions designed to evaluate Pop's recollection ability. Dr. Michaels recited a list of items and asked Pop to say them back to him. He struggled to do so. When asked to repeat them backward, he was unable to. Ten minutes later, Pop couldn't recall even one of the listed items.

Finally, Dr. Michaels clicked his pen closed. "Well, that was extremely helpful. I tend to agree with Dr. Cannon's initial assessment. There is a level of impairment going on. However, the issue before us is a very complicated one. Additional tests should shed some important light on what we're dealing with."

He went on to explain the medical process was a little like a puzzle. "The entire picture isn't clear until all the pieces are in place." He stood and clapped his hands. "So, let's get with it, shall we? We'll run a battery of important physical tests, and when we have the results, I suspect we'll know a whole lot more."

"Will we have results today?" Grace asked.

The doctor stepped near, placed his hand on her shoulder. "Well, sometimes these labs are a little backed up. It appears I pull a little weight around here, and so we've been moved to the front of the line." He grinned at her with assurance.

That seemed to cement his Dr. Michaels's merit in this mother's mind. "Thank you. That's—well, our family appreciates everything you're doing for Wylie."

Ms. Reynolds reappeared and led Wylie out. "You can wait

here, but I suggest the waiting room at the end of the hall. There's coffee and a television. I think you'll be more comfortable."

Over the following hours, Rhett and his family sat and waited while Wylie was tested.

"Mama, do you want me to go get you some lunch?" Leila offered.

Grace shook her head. "No, I can't eat right now." She returned to staring out the window.

Jared threw Rhett a look Rhett could only decipher as disgust. There was no mistaking his younger brother still felt Rhett had overstepped and was responsible for their mother's obvious angst.

Rhett understood. He, too, was anxious about what the findings might reveal. The internet provided a plethora of information, not all of it comforting. Of course, he had to keep reminding himself it was important not to assume every piece of information out there applied to his father's situation. That was a dangerous road that could lead to unnecessary despair. On the other hand, there was also clear indication that waiting to properly assess and treat what appeared to be a cognitive decline in his father's mental function also had negative consequences. Even if seen as the villain in this situation, he had done the right thing.

Several hours passed before Ms. Reynolds appeared and invited them back to Dr. Michaels's office, where the doctor sat behind his desk, alone.

Grace's face darkened with worry. "Where's Wylie?"

Dr. Michaels gave her a reassuring look. "Your husband is resting in another room. They are bringing him dinner while I speak to you privately.

Rhett's gut clenched. Before he could open his mouth to speak, Jared ran his hand through the top of his hair, asking the question on Rhett's mind. "Then, it's bad?"

"Well, it's extremely good that we've assessed Wylie and can establish a plan."

The statement might normally give Rhett some level of pleasure. He had been vindicated. But he could take no pleasure in the look on the doctor's face. Bad news was coming. He braced himself.

Dr. Michaels invited them to all take a seat so he could further explain. "We put Wylie through a number of significant tests today—an MRI, CT scans, and neuroscience brain mapping. We ran a series of blood cultures and further evaluated his cognitive state, including some special tests designed to establish his mental state. Patients suffering from dementia often struggle with various levels of psychopathologies, like depression and anger. And we ran tests to rule out other contributing factors, such as vitamin deficiencies or Lyme Disease."

"What did you find?" Rhett asked.

"While there is no way to definitively establish the root cause of Wylie's issues, the tests have given us a window into information that has led me to rule out Alzheimer's disease."

Grace immediately buried her face in her hands. "Oh, thank God."

"Then what is it?" Jared demanded. "Why is Pop forgetting things? Like his birthday?" He looked to the others. "Remember, he didn't even remember his birthday party."

Dr. Michaels's expression filled with sympathy. "We have reason to believe Wylie is suffering from what's called Lewy body dementia."

"What's that?" Leila asked, her lip quivering.

Dr. Michaels placed his forearms on his desk and leaned forward. "Lewy body dementia, also known as LBD, is a type of progressive dementia that leads to a decline in thinking, reasoning, and independent function."

Rhett rubbed his sweaty palms across the top of his jeans. "Isn't that what Alzheimer is?"

"The symptoms are very similar, but the variable is the cause. In LBD, abnormal deposits of alpha-synuclein protein damage brain cells over time." Dr. Michaels explained.

"What does all that mean?" Grace asked, wiping at tears.

"It means you made the right decision bringing him to the Brain Institute. Our team is one of the best. We're committed to guiding your family through this diagnosis and what is ahead." He leaned back in his chair. "Dementia is an umbrella that covers many types of cognitive digression. Now that we have determined the likely cause, there are many medical trials and medications we can offer that will be very effective."

"In curing our dad?" Leila asked.

"There is no cure," Jared said quietly, staring at the carpet while leaning over with his forearms on his knees.

"I'm afraid he's right. The interventions we offer won't be a cure, but will serve in slowing the progression. For the patient, having dementia is like Christmas lights in your brain begin to flicker and then eventually go out. With medical intervention, we'll slow the number of lights that cease to operate." He paused, letting them take in what he'd said. "Nobody wakes up the day after diagnosis and is at end stage. This disease is a progression. The right meds can slow down the advancement. Our job is to find the right combination. Wylie will be able to do many of the same things he's always done, he'll just do them differently which means figuring out how to overcome the obstacles."

He focused his attention on Grace, the way her hands trembled while folded in her lap. "When our patients encounter a bump in the road, they have two choices. They can move forward or stay stuck. In layman's terms, having dementia feels like making a list of everything you can do and then crossing a few items off every few months. Our job is to help Wylie slow the number of items he has to cross off."

"I—I'm not sure I can..." Her voice drifted off as emotions overtook her composure.

Seated beside Rhett, his mother's face crumpled before she dropped her face into her hands and sobbed.

14

None of them spoke while crossing the lobby and walking across the parking lot out to their cars. Clearly, each of them was trying to absorb the mountain of information provided and settle the fear that came with this diagnosis. There were so many details, and many more possibilities than probabilities.

They learned the rate of progression for Lewy's varied widely. On average, people with this disease lived between three and eleven years after diagnosis, but some survived twenty years or more. The degree of impairment at diagnosis could affect life expectancy.

After meeting with the family, Dr. Michaels brought in Wylie and delivered the news. The doctor explained Wylie was considered to be in stage three of seven levels of decline. He'd suffered memory loss, though still somewhat mild. There were changes in his ability to concentrate and make decisions. While still able to function normally from a physical standpoint, it wouldn't be long before impairment would start—tremors, risk of falling, and even the possibility of choking. The projected symptoms were sobering.

Rhett learned that some of the information was already known to his parents. While their understanding had been sketchy, they had sought out additional information on their own prior to today. Rhett suspected Jared had orchestrated some of that, and the idea he'd been cut out of the process earlier continued to anger him.

Given Pop's future, that was over. Starting today.

Deep inside, Rhett knew he could never return to Chicago, at least not for some time. Sure, the decision would come at severe personal cost—staying longer than he'd intended already had—but what choice did he have? There would never be an instance where he would turn his back and not be here to support his parents when they needed him most.

Rhett tried not to think of the distant future, of what a world without Pop would look like. He couldn't stomach the thought of the man he so admired being reduced to— Well, he simply couldn't go there.

What he could focus on was making sure his family and the business his dad had fought to build were secure. The oyster farm needed strong leadership and would require financial direction. Emotional support for his mother and sister would be essential over the coming months. Even Jared, if the kid cared to admit it, could bear some brotherly support from someone who could keep him on a firm foundation.

Time would tell if his brother would walk on his own two feet without using chemical crutches to journey this hard path. Rhett's money was on the idea the past would repeat and everything would fall on Rhett to shoulder—just as it always had.

The first thing Rhett attended to the following morning was to get out his laptop and type out his resignation letter. Every keystroke caused him to wince. It wasn't easy to bid goodbye to a position he'd spent years cultivating, working long and arduous hours, giving up relationships and a lot of sleep in order to attain the respect and admiration of all in the financial industry—not only in Chicago, but nationwide.

Of course, Judith Sandidge's recent decision had eased him into the idea of moving on from the company. Never had Rhett imagined taking an extended sabbatical and leaving the entire financial industry, even temporarily. Rhett swallowed against the lump building in his throat and hit send on the email without knowing when he'd be able to collect the pieces of the life he'd known and step on the treadmill back to success.

The next thing that needed attention was his place in Chicago. He reached out to Joyce Mintzas, the leasing agent who had helped him secure a coveted flat in an up-and-coming area filled with restaurants, shops and lively bars.

Not that he spent a lot of time there—he had a cot and a shower at the office and spent most of his time flying—but it was still his place. Joyce would secure a suitable tenant to sublet who would appreciate the fact it came completely furnished. Her firm even offered to pack up his personal belongings and move them to storage, canceling the need for him to make a trip back.

With the urgent tasks now accomplished, Rhett closed his laptop and headed downstairs to find the house empty. "Mom?" he called out. "Pop?"

It was then that he noticed his parents standing out on the lawn. His mother's head was folded against Pop's shoulder, and he was gently patting her back and whispering something against her ear.

The sight squeezed his heart, and he had to look away. His parents were two of the strongest human beings on the planet. Seeing them like this—so reduced by their circumstances—caused Rhett to choke back the onset of tears. He cleared his throat, swallowed hard, and pulled his phone from his pocket.

He scrolled past Ben's name in his contacts, pausing briefly at Cam's name before thumbing on down until he landed on Diane. He took a deep breath and pressed dial.

She picked up on the second ring. "Hello?"

There was a lightness in her voice and instantly, he felt better. "Hey, Diane. It's me, Rhett. You have time to meet me somewhere and talk?"

HE WAS unsure why he felt the need to reach out to Diane, why he hadn't asked Cam and Ben to meet him and throw down a few beers. The only answer he could come up with was that in the short time they'd spent reconnecting, he'd learned Diane was a great listener. Spouting his troubles was certainly not his style. Still, he needed to talk to someone. Besides, he wasn't in the mood to yuck it up with the guys. Not to mention the fact Rhett didn't want the details out there just yet. His parents deserved privacy while they wrapped their heads around this new reality.

For now, he'd keep the details of Pop's diagnosis quiet. Upon his urging, Jared and Leila had agreed. Pop was a proud man. He wouldn't want the entire town knowing what he suffered and what was ahead. He was no victim. The smaller circle of those who knew, the better. At least for now.

Diane suggested they meet at the Ebb Tide Nursing Home out on the lawn. She volunteered twice a week.

The veracity of his immediate negative response surprised even him. "I'm sorry. It's just—well, I'd rather meet somewhere a little—"

Diane broke into his explanation. "No worries. We can meet where ever you like."

He could hear something in her voice, confusion—or, perhaps a bit of judgment? It wasn't like that. How could he possibly explain he had nothing against hanging around the residents of Ebb Tide? That was most certainly *not* how he felt. He simply couldn't—well, how could he watch those people, knowing that same full-time nursing care was likely in his father's future?

He'd rather chew on broken seashells.

They agreed to meet at her place. "I'll fix us a bite of lunch," she told him. Then, as if sensing his mood and the need to be alone, she added, "Stacy is helping my mother out at the Whale Museum today. We'll have the place to ourselves."

Diane lived at the end of Starfish Lane, the road that extended past New Hope Church. Her modest house was light yellow with a covered porch and white shutters, tucked on a tiny plot surrounded by a thicket of pine trees and ferns.

Rhett pulled into the driveway and parked. He glanced in the rearview mirror, amazed at how tired he appeared. He'd had a few sleepless nights lately, and the lack of rest had taken its toll.

Diane's sidewalk was lined with flowers. He wasn't sure of the names, but he recognized some as being the ones his mother had planted in the pots outside the doors leading to the retail store at their place out on the bay—brightly colored petunias and marigolds and tiny blue flowers his mother called lobelia. He stifled a chuckle, surprised he could recall that insignificant fact. He'd never considered the gift of being able to store and recall information, until recently.

Rhett climbed the steps onto the small covered porch and lightly rapped on the white door. It instantly opened and he was met with the image of Diane standing there wiping her hands on a dishtowel.

"Come in," she said, motioning him inside with a bright smile. She wore white jeans and a T-shirt tucked loosely at her waist. She looked beautiful, standing there with her blonde hair tied back. "I hope you like crab salad. I'm afraid it's all I had."

"No worries," he assured her. "I didn't give you a lot of notice. And, yes. I love crab salad." Already, he felt lighter. Just being out...away from the house and the heaviness they all felt.

She closed the door behind him. "I set the table on the back deck. The weather's lovely today, and I thought we'd take advantage of the sunshine."

He nodded and followed her outside. But not before eyeing the inside of her home. It was a sensible place, uncluttered and nicely decorated. In the main living area, she had comfortable sofas facing each other. A square coffee table was planted in the center of a large rug. A bowl of shells was nestled on top of the table next to a couple of pillar candles and a small stack of books. He couldn't make out the titles, but her reading habits looked to lean toward books about nature. Not entirely surprising. When they'd met for a quick bite the other night, he'd recognized there was something different about her. Knowing what she'd been through and that she'd survived—well, he admired her for that.

Built-in shelves flanked a fireplace made of river rock. Diane displayed framed photos of her daughter, of her mother, and many coastal shots that could have been taken by a professional. He pointed. "You take those?"

She glanced where he indicated and grinned. "I did. In rehab, they urge you to find a hobby to focus on when the struggle to drink rears its ugly head. I'm getting pretty good, even if I say so myself. I guess that means I struggle more than I like." She granted him another one of those smiles, the ones that could warm even the coldest soul.

"You still struggle?" he asked, then immediately kicked himself for prying into her personal issues.

His asking didn't seem to bother her. "I'll always struggle," she admitted. "Now, I have tools to cope. I no longer have to escape my feelings by tossing back a shot of vodka." She looked at him with eyes that were as deep and blue as the ocean. "I do miss a good margarita once in a while. Yet I've never been more at peace. It's a wonderful feeling really."

Her unabashed confession of wrong paths taken, of healing from her former need to anesthetize emotions, pulled at him.

Until recently, he'd had it all together. Life was good. He had a great career, money, respect. While he had never married or had children, he was part of a family he steadfastly loved.

Events outside his control were now pulling that security rug out from underneath his feet. Frankly, while he wouldn't admit it as freely as Diane, his foundation was shifting. Often, he worried he might tumble, and he didn't know how to keep himself upright. Especially when his mind wandered to the possibilities and what was projected to be ahead for his dad. Dementia would rob Pop of everything. How was Rhett supposed to accept the fact the man he loved most on this earth would eventually lose his memory—may not even remember Rhett at some point.

The idea made him shudder. He swallowed, shook off the emotion. He was the rock in the family. He couldn't crumble.

Diane invited him to sit while she returned inside for the food. In minutes, she reappeared with plates in hand. She set them on the placemats and then took her seat. "So, I was surprised to get your call," she admitted. "But, happy."

Warmth pooled in Rhett's gut. He'd made the right decision in reaching out. He needed some of that peace she claimed to have. "Wow. This looks great." He picked up his fork.

The image of his mom and dad embracing out on the lawn earlier suddenly popped inside his mind. His folks had been married nearly forty years. How were they supposed to deal with this?

Their deep love for one another was written in their eyes, woven into their souls—like they were always meant to be united and nothing could ever tear them apart.

Until this.

He held the fork mid-air, overcome with feelings he couldn't even name. His face reddened as unbidden tears formed. He angrily blinked—once, twice, three times—trying to collect himself and gain control.

She noticed.

"Rhett, are you okay?" She dropped her own fork and reached across the table, took his hand in hers, and gave it a light squeeze. "I'm here if you want to talk about it."

He wiped at his forehead, embarrassed. It took several long breaths before he could speak. When he could, he forced himself to look her in the eyes. "I'm—well, our family got some bad news this week."

Her eyebrows drew together with concern. "Oh, Rhett. No."

He nodded. "Yes, my dad. I think I mentioned the other night that he's been having trouble with his memory. Has had for some time, actually."

Rhett told Diane about the signs he'd noticed—how he'd opened the cupboard door to find a carton of milk. How his mother had gotten flustered and claimed to have done it herself. He drew a deep breath and told her about the visit to Portland and the horrible diagnosis. "I don't understand why. It appears my family kept me in the dark and didn't want me to know."

She nodded with understanding. "Denial can be a huge motivator. Sometimes we find mentally blocking out bad things is far more attractive than admitting the truth and handling the consequences." She slowly released his hand. "Knowing your mother, she also wanted to protect her children from the news."

"Jared and Leila both knew. Well, I'm unsure how much my sister was aware, but Jared definitely was inside the loop. He'd even taken Pop to Astoria to see Dr. Cannon."

"The fact they elected not to call and tell you leaves you feeling left out." She made the statement without any judgment. Her ability to assess the situation, even when not flattering on his part, was comforting.

Rhett nodded. "We both know Dr. Cannon is a great family physician. He's served as our family doctor. He's the one who set my broken leg when I fell off my bike in the fifth grade. He's a capable physician, but he's no expert. Especially when it comes to neurological deficits in the brain. Pop should've seen specialists long ago. It wasn't until I made arrangements that he was properly evaluated. I even had to fight my family to get him there." Rhett knew he was spilling more than intended, but the release felt good. Telling Diane felt like an anchor being pulled from somewhere inside him, liberating him from the burden he'd been carrying. Even if only slightly.

"People do the best they can," she offered. "As much as we like to think we can appoint motives to the things people do, especially those things that hurt us...well, only God really knows the heart. Your family loves you, Rhett. Despite failing to act how you wished they had, I am certain hiding your father's illness wasn't meant to cause you pain. Perhaps they simply didn't want you to worry until they knew more." She gave him a weak smile. "Regardless, you'll need to forgive them. That's the only way to release the hold their withholding the truth has on you."

She tossed her head back and laughed. "Do you know how often I had to rehearse the twelve steps in order to make peace with my own mother?"

Rhett knew the wisdom of what she'd said. Of course, he had to forgive them. Forgetting would be a whole other story.

"I know that look," she teased. "Been there, done that." She held up four fingers. "And I have the husbands to prove it. You'll wrestle with all this, but in the end, think carefully about what I've said. Holding onto grudges only causes you pain and drives deeper wedges between you and the ones you love."

Rhett inhaled sharply, and his eyebrows lifted. "So, tell me, Diane. How did you get so wise?"

"By attending the School of Hard Knocks," she pointed out. "And I haven't yet graduated. Thinking of going for my masters." She paused, gave him a meaningful look. "Don't follow my lead, Rhett. Learn from my mistakes."

She may be right, of course. His lips twitched with a wide smile as he joined her in laughing about life and its troubles. He only wished he could face adversity as well as her.

"I know what your family is facing is terribly difficult. I'm so very sorry. But, Rhett—you can't control any of this. The only thing you can do is wake up every day and do the best you can. Be kind, and don't expect anything more of yourself. Don't expect to do everything perfectly. And don't expect that of others. It's just not how it works."

He felt the burn at the back of his eyes again. "How do you do that?" he asked. "How do you make me feel better simply by —well, by being so understanding?"

"Listening is a powerful thing. Few people know how to put their own stuff aside and really focus on another person. It's taken me a lot of practice to get better at the effort. And a lot of counseling." She did it again, smiled at him in a way that made him tingle inside.

Diane cast her eyes heavenward. "You should have seen me a year ago. In ways, I don't even feel like the same person. Back then, my need to control—well, everything—had created this vacuum where my soul had once lived." She looked away, far out over the yard and the tall pines beyond. "I'm more like my real self now. I can see that. But I sure walked a bumpy road to get here."

Rhett was quiet for a few moments, letting the sea air and the sun work on him.

Diane pushed her plate away and propped her elbow on the table. "You know..." She rested her chin on her upturned palm. "I've never really assessed my life like I just did. Thanks for that."

"I came for selfish reasons," he admitted. "I'm glad this talk wasn't completely one-sided."

When they'd finished eating, Rhett helped her bring the dishes inside. "Thanks again. That crab was delicious. Better than most restaurants." He moved for the dishwasher.

"Don't you dare!" she warned. "I don't let my lunch guests do the dishes."

"Is that so?" he said, noticing how well she'd aged. Or, not aged. She looked nearly the same as she had in high school, back when he'd gazed at her from his locker. She still wore her blonde hair long and loose around her shoulders, though today she'd tied it back. Her eyes still seemed to twinkle when she smiled. And her mouth—well, she had nice lips. That's all he'd best say about that.

She followed him out when it was time for him to go. At his car, he turned so they faced each other "I know I said it, but I do appreciate everything. The lunch, and especially the talk. I needed it." Before she could respond, he decided to add, "It was a good date."

Her eyebrows shot up. "You thought this was a date?"

He grinned, surprised at the sudden turn in this conversation at his instigation. "Not at first."

She placed her hands on her hips, smiled back at him. "Well, news flash. I've given up dating."

"Gonna grow old all alone, eh?" he teased, hardly able to keep from laughing. He offered a short, good-natured perusal of her from head to toe. "I don't see that for your future, Diane."

She smirked, seeming to enjoy the banter. "See it or not, that's the plan. Now, I admit I might change my mind in twenty years or so. But for now, I'm single and happy. The husband parade is officially disbanded. No dating. No men," she added for emphasis.

"Probably a smart decision." He leaned close enough to smell the light fragrance in her hair and whispered against her ear, "Kind of a waste, though." Then, without even planning to, he dropped a light kiss on the flesh of her earlobe.

A tiny smile lifted the corner of her lips. "I am open to being friends, though."

He took a full step back and reached out a hand for her to shake.

She laughed, rolled her eyes, and shook his hand.

Rhett couldn't seem to wipe the goofy grin from his face as he said, "Friends, it is. For now."

15

Upon returning home, Rhett walked in the door and headed for the kitchen. There were no signs of life, so Rhett made his way to the store. Before he even got up the steps, he spied his mother behind the counter, ringing up an order for some customers—what looked to be a man, his wife, and their two small children.

His mom came from around the counter, bent and offered the two kiddos a treat out of her bowl of chocolate-covered blackberries. She often said she sold as many packages of the sweet candy as she did the packages of smoked oysters.

Rhett turned the knob and pulled the door open. A tiny bell tinkled above the door. "Hey," he said.

The guy was dressed in pressed khaki shorts and a button-down shirt rolled up at the elbows. A tourist down from Seattle, Rhett guessed. The man grinned at him and held up a package of purchased oysters. "Listen, man. You've got to try these. Seriously delicious. Just a hint of smoke, briny, and clean tasting."

Yup, definitely from Seattle.

Rhett nodded. "Yes, I agree. Some of the best I've ever eaten." He and his mother exchanged a meaningful glance.

"Well, c'mon, kids. We don't want to waste this beautiful day." He glanced over at Rhett. "We're heading to the Whale Museum. I heard it's very educational."

Rhett nodded. "Yeah, it's a great place to take children."

"Oh, yes," his mother said. "Ellen Jeffers is the proprietor and is so knowledgeable. She's a friend. Just tell her you've just been over here at the oyster farm, and she'll give you special treatment." She winked.

"Thank you," the woman said. "We will."

When they'd gone, Rhett joined his mom behind the counter. He leaned and kissed her cheek. "How are you, Mom?"

She sighed. "I've been better. I got on the internet last night. Boy howdy, wrong move. The information out there will scare you to pieces." She shook her head. "I think we're going to just have to follow Dr. Michaels's instructions and take this thing a day at a time."

Rhett hugged his mother's shoulders. "I think that's wise. Remember what we were told. Nobody wakes up the day after diagnosis and is at end stage. Pop's disease will be a progression of symptoms. He's strong and determined. We have every hope he will move through the stages slowly."

Rhett paused, briefly considering the timing of his announcement. He decided he might as well go ahead. "I resigned my position in Chicago."

Her face immediately wore her sadness. "Oh, Rhett. No." She vehemently shook her head. "You can't do that. You mustn't place your life—the career you worked so hard for—on hold."

He held up a hand to stop her.

Instead of complying, she grasped his hand with surprising force. "That's exactly what we feared, why we didn't tell you."

He pulled back. "That's why?"

His mother brushed some chocolate crumbs from the top of the glass display case and moved the bowl of candy back in place. "Yes. It was not hard to figure you'd upend everything and try to take over."

Seeing the hurt on his face, she immediately added, "Oh, that's not what I meant." She waved off her comment. "I only meant that your sense of keen sense of responsibility would take front and center. This is not your burden to carry, son."

"What? You think you can shoulder all this alone?" he countered.

"We have Jared here," she argued. "And your sister."

The door opened, and his brother strode in. "What about me?"

Their mother let out a patient sigh. "I was just telling your brother that you would help with everything here. That Rhett didn't need to leave his job and move home."

"What?" Jared turned his gaze to Rhett, his expression dark. "You're moving home?"

"Well, yeah," Rhett admitted. "I mean, what with everything—"

"That's stupid! I know you think no one but you can make good decisions. How could your brother, the muck-up, possibly handle what has to be done?"

Rhett offered a noncommittal one-shouldered shrug. "I didn't say that."

Jared took a step toward him, his hands fisting at his sides. "Really? Because it seems to me you've been saying that since you got here, if not in words, certainly in actions."

Rhett worked the muscle in his jaw.

Jared angrily ran his hand through the top of his hair. "After all, how can the guy who never lived up to your expectations handle Pop's medical situation or keep this family going when His Highness, the Smart One isn't around to make sure we're all dancing to the right tune?"

Before Rhett could defend himself further, Jared spun around and grabbed the doorknob.

Their mother split her glances between her two warring sons. "Jared, wait. Where are you going? Let's talk this through," she pleaded.

His younger brother turned, paused. "Don't worry, Mom. I'm fine. Really."

"But where are you going?" she repeated.

"I'm going to a meeting. A very much-needed meeting." And with that, Jared headed out the door, letting it slam behind him.

Rhett's mother turned on him. "Son, you have to back off of him. He's trying, and the added pressure you're placing on him is not good for his sobriety. He needs our support—all of our support, including yours."

Rhett pointed after him. "The guy who needs all the support is somehow equipped to run the business? Come on, Mom. Think."

Her mouth pursed tightly as her chin lifted. "You haven't been here. Jared's right. You are not uniquely qualified to decide what's best for the family or the business. He's been working alongside your father for some time. In your absence, he's shown himself more than capable." Each word was slow, meticulous, and hit its target—his heart—with deft accuracy. "Rhett Daniel, you know I love you with all my heart. But it's past time you lay this ill-placed judgment of your brother aside."

Her remarks smarted. Rhett hadn't been scolded like that since—well, since he'd stayed out all night with Ben and Cam the night they graduated and had failed to call her to let her know he was okay.

Rhett ran his hand through his hair. He was trying to do the right thing here. Did either of them have any idea what this decision had cost him? Regardless of what they thought, even if Jared was now on the straight and narrow, he was not capable of running this entire operation without help. Who else was going to step in and provide the needed leadership, the financial direction? Who had the ability to step in for Pop and develop a business strategy that would help weather the storm?

Did Jared have a master's in finance? Did Leila? And, never mind his sister's worthless husband. He was more interested in a bag of potato chips than on cash ratios or return on investment data.

Neither his mother nor his brother must be aware of how often he and Pop talked, how much Pop already relied on his input and advice. Sure, Jared knew the day-to-day operation. But no one in the family was in a better position to step in and run this oyster farm from a financial standpoint and keep it thriving. No one but him.

Given that, Rhett had stepped up and done what was required. He'd taken a leave from the financial world and had committed to support his family, no matter the personal cost.

Question was, how had he become the bad guy?

16

Rhett returned to the house in a huff, trying to calm down. Diane said he had to learn to forgive his family, and he was trying—truly he was. Never mind how much their words stung.

Inside, he slung his jacket on the back of the sofa and went immediately to his dad's office. He slid into his father's chair and logged onto the computer to check his emails.

As expected, there was one from Judith.

Rhett – While I am sorry to learn of your decision, I accept your resignation and wish you all the best in your endeavors in Oregon. ~ Judith

Rhett leaned back, stunned.

That was it? After pouring countless hours and his blood, sweat and tears into that firm, that's what he got? What amounted to a swift kick disguised as a pat on the back as he headed out the door?

He buried his chin in his hands and rubbed at his beard stubble. He felt like a kid who had opened a Christmas package hoping for the newest Xbox, only to find he'd been presented with a hand-held pinball machine.

He'd definitely been taking his gut punches lately. Frankly, he was tired of getting kicked around.

Rhett shoved the chair back with force. He stood and marched through the house and out the back door leading to the oyster sheds. That's when he noticed Ben's truck pulling into the yard. Inside, Cam sat on the passenger side.

Ben parked, and both his buddies climbed out. Cam gave a wave. "Hey, Rhett. We came to kidnap you."

Without a moment's consideration, Rhett shook his head. "Can't. I've got a lot on my plate, guys."

"Nonsense," Ben argued. "A bunch of us are gathering on the field behind the high school for a friendly game of football. We don't take no for an answer. Besides, you're on vacation, and what can a little fun hurt?"

Rhett didn't want to let on that there was anything wrong. Neither did he feel like messing around with the guys right now. Something in their eyes told him he would have a hard time saying no, that they both meant business. If he tried to argue, it'd lead to him spilling—and he wasn't ready for them to know. Eventually, he'd have to admit the diagnosis and everything that meant for his pop. But, not today. He didn't have the emotional reserves it'd take to admit his life had just been upended—both personally and professionally.

"Look, guys—" He held up open palms, deciding to at least give declining their invitation a try. "I know you mean well, and all. But—"

Ben slapped him on the back. "No, buts. It's team reunion time."

They linked arms with Rhett and pulled him towards the truck, barely allowing him time to text his mom that he'd be gone for a bit.

The football field was located directly behind the high school. As soon as they pulled into the empty parking lot, memories flooded Rhett's mind—images of this lot filled with cars and pickups, of the ballfield lit up and lined with bleachers filled with rowdy townspeople, all cheering. He could see cheerleaders at the edge of the field in short skirts waving pom-poms. He could hear the thumping of the high school band music and see old Mr. Parker waving his small white baton to the beat as he walked backward across the fifty-yard line.

Rhett could feel the adrenaline rising in the locker room where he and his best buds had crashed helmets and yelled into one another's faces, readying to challenge their enemy. Nothing else in his life had that same feel, that mix of sweat and expectation, that blend of fire and freedom.

Man, no wonder those were called the glory days. He'd been too young to care about the physical consequences of slamming into a hundred-and-eighty-pound opponent on the field but old enough to care about the long string of girls who wanted to date a varsity first-string varsity player.

How long had it been since he'd thought about any of this? There were guys who never left those football hero days and recounted the stories over and over, but not Rhett. Like so much of his formative years, he'd put this on a mental shelf as he moved on in life, letting work and contracts and rising to the top of his chosen field become more important than memories and friends and family.

Autumn Friday nights in Pacific Bay were—and had always been—reserved for football. The residents were all in, whether they had kids playing or not. No one missed a game.

"Duvall has the ball and runs it! Going...going...and we have a touchdown!"

The past swept Rhett up and carried him to a place in his head that was filled with warm recollections of a time when life was simple, and exciting, and filled with community. The youth in the Chicago suburbs had no idea what it was like to grow up in a town like this, where everyone knew everyone else and neighbors supported neighbors.

If he ever had kids—yes, he was climbing on forty and that wasn't likely—he would want them raised in a community with the kind of support growing up in Pacific Bay offered him and his friends and siblings.

Ben cut the engine and turned to Rhett. "You ready to kick some butt?"

Feeling like a kid again, Rhett grinned and knuckle-punched his buddy. "Cougar power."

On the field were several guys he recognized from high school. Matt Reynard, who had been their kicker. Jason Cunningham, the half-back. Hansel Stack, the top blocker in the Pacific Northwest back in the day.

After a few shoulder punches and some pats on the back, the guys all got down to business.

Despite being years older, they still had it going. Sure, they ran a little slower. Their blocks packed a little less power. But for old guys, the effort was impressive. Of course, they'd pay for the fun when they woke to joint pains and muscle aches. It didn't matter; the time spent on the field provided all of them much needed exertion of pent-up energy and, frankly, just a lot of good, old-fashioned fun.

They stumbled off the field, tired but wearing wide grins.

"So, who's up for a beer?" Hansel asked. "I have a cooler in the back of my truck."

This caused a wave of laughter. Some things never changed.

Jason and Hansel carried the cooler to the edge of the field, and they all grabbed a bottle and found a place on the bleachers.

"It's good to see you back in town," Matt remarked. He twisted the top off his bottle and lifted it to his mouth, taking a long draw.

"It's good to be back," Rhett said, taking a longneck from Hansel. He clinked his bottle against the one Ben was holding. "It's been great to see you all again."

He learned Hansel's wife had beat breast cancer a few years back. Jason's car dealership in Portland was flourishing, and he was thinking of expanding into Eugene. He lived there full-time now, but after his divorce, he bought a house back in Pacific Bay and spent weekends in his hometown. "Where I can square my head and leave all the stress behind," he told them.

Matt's son was now the quarterback on the Cougar team. "Yeah, he's natural," his dad said with pride.

Cam nodded. "No offense, Rhett. But people claim he's the best QB the town ever had."

Matt grinned. "Yeah, looks like we're not going to have to foot the bill for that kid's schooling. Now, his sister—well, that's another story. She has it in her head to go to Stanford. Wants to be an engineer."

"Stanford's a good school," Rhett said, resting his bottle of beer against the top of his leg. "The engineering school has a stellar reputation. When she graduates, reach out to me. I've worked with a lot of clients in the San Francisco area. Maybe I can help her make some connections."

"That's great, man. Thanks!" Matt reached in the cooler for another beer. "Any help would be appreciated."

"So, when are you heading back?" Jason asked.

Rhett paused, unsure just how to answer. "Well, actually, I've decided to stay for awhile." He took a deep breath. There would be no withholding the news forever, nor would he be able to keep the reason why a secret. Still, he wasn't ready to come clean—at least not until his entire family agreed to share news about Pop's condition. Moreover, it was his dad's decision when he might be ready. Dr. Michaels said it could be some time before his condition worsened to the point where others would know and understand Pop was dealing with mental decline.

Rhett let his gaze drift across the faces of his buddies. "It's like this. I'm ready to take a break from the rat race. Like Jason,

I'm ready to reduce the stress in my life, step back, and enjoy myself a bit. Even more, I'm realizing my folks are aging, and I haven't been able to spend the kind of time with them I really want lately. I don't want to wake up one day to the 'call,' the one that you dread. If, and when, I lose one of my parents, I don't want to live with regret." He swirled the remaining beer in his bottle. "I'm more than good, financially. I'm at the top of my game in my career. So, the way I figured, I could afford to take a break, recalibrate. When I'm ready, I'll return and pick back up where I left off." From the looks on their faces, his answer was satisfactory. His response was the truth. At least, in part.

Hansel nodded and removed the top from his second bottle. "Look, I think that's a wise move. Sometimes, you don't get second chances to spend time with the people you cherish. When they're gone, they're gone. I got a reprieve when my wife beat her cancer, and I don't plan to waste the gift I was given. I'm not afraid to admit I've made Gayle a priority. No matter the cost, I make time for her. I'm even planning to take her to Maui for her upcoming birthday instead of buying a new truck this year." He rubbed the side of his chin. "Don't let that out. It's a surprise."

Jason gave his shoulder a squeeze. "That's great, man. She's going to love it."

Rhett smiled to himself. These guys were no longer the girl-crazed jocks he knew from high school. Of course, neither was he. One of the benefits of remaining in Pacific Bay was reconnecting and spending time with his friends. That, and getting to know Diane Jeffers much better.

His phone buzzed in his pocket. At the same time, Cam's phone rang.

They both pulled the phones out and to their ears.

"Hey, Leila. What's up?" Rhett asked. His sister rarely called him.

"Rhett! Get home!" she said, her voice frantic. "Dad's

missing."

17

It took less than an hour for searchers to assemble at the shoreline at the mouth of the bay leading to the inlet where the Pacific Bay Oyster farm was located. After learning that Wylie's boat had been discovered empty and drifting nearby this location, Cameron Davis had launched a full-on search effort by the U.S. Coast Guard. He was the commanding officer at the local office and charged with the responsibility for sea rescues up and down the coastline.

In addition, an impressive group of locals assembled to join in the effort. Craig Anthony donated his fishing fleet and employees, as did Allie. Captain Paul was the first to arrive on the scene, ready to take *Reel Chances* out to aid in the search for Wylie.

Rhett's heart pounded as he stood by, feeling helpless. His mother and sister reported that they had not seen Wylie in well over an hour when they received a telephone call from a local crab boat fisherman telling them Wylie's boat had been found floating just offshore, but with no one on board. Wylie's wallet was on the table inside the small cuddy cabin, suggesting he'd been on board, at least at some point. The engine was not running, and a tether rope was tied to the bow and left drifting in the waves. The question was, did he fall overboard?

Jared approached, running. "Rhett! Where is he? Where's Pop?" he hollered.

Rhett rubbed his forehead, and his heart squeezed. "We don't know." He updated his brother and told him what they'd found. "Where's Mom and sis?"

"They stayed back at the house, just in case."

"In case?"

"In case..." Rhett let his voice drift off. He couldn't say it. Couldn't dare to think it, even.

Jared grabbed at Rhett's shoulder. "Why are we just standing here? Let's go help them."

Rhett shook his head. "Cam's got it covered out there. He said we'd only be in the way. I don't like it, but—"

"That's crazy!" Jared barked. "I'm going."

Rhett grabbed his brother's arm. "Use your head, bro. What do you think you can do that Cam and the highly trained search team aren't already doing? There are over a dozen boats scanning the shoreline. Two helicopters are searching. We need to stay put."

Jared took hold of Rhett's shoulders and pulled him close, clung to him, "Rhett, Pop's out there in the water somewhere." His voice shook with emotion.

Rhett drew a tight breath and gave his brother a hug. "They'll find him," he promised, though he knew his words were hollow. He didn't know any such thing. What he did know is that his mind couldn't begin to grasp the aspect of danger facing them. He couldn't entertain the idea of his dad succumbing to the dark, gray water—the icy-cold temperatures that would overtake him in a very short time. The possibility they might never find his body if—

Rhett violently shook his head. No! He wouldn't go there.

The following hour drug by slowly, like watching drops of

molasses falling into a gallon jar and waiting for those drops to finally fill the container. Earlier, Rhett had been joking around with the guys on the field, never knowing his father was in perilous danger. How could he not have sensed something was awry? Could his beloved father have drawn his last breath and Rhett not felt it deep inside?

"Rhett!"

He turned to face the familiar voice. Diane ran across the sand to join him. When she'd neared, he could see her face was fraught with worry. "Rhett, do you know anything yet?"

He shook his head. "No. Nothing." Out of habit, he glanced at his wristwatch. "We should've heard something by now."

"Mom's heading out to be with your mom and sister. Stacey, too."

"Thanks, I appreciate that. They shouldn't be alone."

Diane gave his arm a squeeze. "They aren't alone. Susan Wilson and Linda Pullen are already there. A lot of people are scanning the nearby woods, too, just in case." She lifted her chin slightly. "I hope you aren't angry, but I told. I explained about Wylie."

Rhett felt the breath leave his lungs. The news wasn't entirely welcome, but how could he possibly be angry with her? Given the situation, she'd done the right thing, and he told her so.

"How are you?" She leaned her head against his shoulder. "I've been praying, Rhett. This is awful."

Pastor Riggin and his son, Nolan, appeared. Followed by Axel, the owner down at the Sea Star Tavern. "Yes, we're all praying," Pastor Riggin told Rhett. "The church's prayer chain was activated the minute we heard. Axel, here, heads it up."

Axel nodded enthusiastically. "We've seen some amazing answers to prayer," he acknowledged. When a call for prayer goes out, even the guys down at the tavern drop their beers to the counter and bow their heads with folded hands."

Rhett thanked them both, then turned his attention back to the gray, angry waves and the boats in the distance. That's when his phone rang.

He immediately pulled it to his ear without bothering to identify the caller. "Yeah?"

"Rhett, it's your mother. They found him. They found Wylie." Relief was evident in her voice.

"They found him? Is he okay?"

"Yes, he appears to be fine."

"Where was he?" Rhett demanded.

"He was discovered wandering the soup aisle down at Bricker's Grocery." He could hear her voice falter as she choked back tears of relief. "Apparently, Wylie took the boat out and got hungry."

A small laugh escaped Rhett's mouth, accompanied by tears of his own. When he looked over at his brother—saw the fear in Jared's bright-blue eyes, Rhett placed a hand on Jared's shoulder to shore him up. "He's fine, Jared. Pop is okay."

A sound escaped from Jared's mouth, something between a laugh and a cry, while tears spilled onto Jared's face. Seconds later, he was reaching for Rhett. For the second time in the span of less than a few hours, the two brothers hugged, each one drawing strength from the other.

Rhett suddenly realized, in that moment, something had changed between them. Jared needed him. For the first time in his life, Rhett also knew that he needed Jared to be strong for him.

18

Rhett and Jared helped Cam secure their dad's abandoned boat, then they both climbed in their respective vehicles and headed home.

Rhett's head was reeling over the events of the past few hours and the implications. His dad was showing signs of the next stage of progression, as described by Dr. Michaels. Pop was now exhibiting increasingly poor judgment and deepening confusion. He'd wandered off to the grocery store, leaving his wallet and forgetting to properly tether the boat—all of which were unsafe decisions and completely uncharacteristic choices for the father he'd always known.

No doubt, Pop's confusion and these difficulties made it unsafe to leave him on his own without supervision. How had they landed here so fast?

Rhett slowed at the turnoff onto the winding road that circled the bay. Despite the chilly air outside, he rolled down the window letting the salt-rich air fill his truck and tried to clear his head.

He'd hoped they'd have time to adjust to the diagnosis before making decisions for his father that he would, no doubt, see as ripping away his freedom. The key would be to pull off the new mode without being obvious. If that was possible.

In light of that, Rhett called a family meeting later that day. While Pop rested, they all gathered around the kitchen table.

Rhett cleared his throat. "So, today was a turning point. I don't know about the rest of you, but this one scared me."

His mom nodded. She leaned her head against Leila's shoulder. "I was terrified," she admitted.

Jared rubbed his chin. "Well, it's clear we can't be leaving Pop alone. He's going to have to be supervised. We can't take the chance he'd do something and hurt himself."

Rhett gripped the edge of the table. "Agreed." He looked to his mom and sister. "How about you two?"

They both slowly nodded.

Over the course of the next hour, they outlined exactly what that would look like and made a plan. There were so many details and decisions.

Leila squeezed her mom's shoulder. "The team at the Brain Institute told us it was important to keep a routine so Pop doesn't get confused."

Their mom dabbed at a tear forming. "Yes, and I want to protect Wylie's dignity at all costs. After today, the news is out. Perhaps that's just as well. At least now, people will be watching out for him."

"That's good, right?"

Their mother smiled at her daughter, weakly. "Yes, but at what cost? He deserves the respect of this family, and of the community where he made his home all these years. *Respect, not pity.*"

Jared patted her hand. "Pop is respected, Mom. A medical diagnosis will never change that."

She nodded, having made her feelings understood. "So, I'll be by his side. When I can't, Leila will need to step in and cover. That doesn't mean you two boys are off the hook. You will have to help, too. As a family, we'll do what Wylie needs and watch over him. Protect him."

"Mom, you and I will have to make a trip to the bank. I think it's wise if we get all the accounts out of Pop's name and make sure he no longer has the ability to make any financial transactions." Rhett caught the brief look Jared cast. He thought of all that Diane had said, and of the embrace he and his brother had exchanged earlier. With a deep breath, he returned the gaze, "Do you agree, Jared?"

His brother raised his eyebrows ever so slightly. "Sure, yeah. That's a good idea."

Rhett released his grip on the table's edge and shoved his chair back. He stood and clapped his hands together. "Great, then all of us are in agreement."

The following morning, Rhett and his mom made a trip to the bank as planned, in order to make the arrangements they'd all determined were in the best interests of Pop, and for the operations of the oyster farm. Pop was no longer capable of managing the money end of things. Thankfully, Rhett had continued to play an advisory role and understood the structure of their operating accounts and all that needed transitioned out of Pop's control.

Charlie Truesdale, the bank manager, greeted them as soon as they entered. "Hey, so sorry to hear about Wylie. Everyone in town was devastated by the news. Who would ever have imagined a person with as much vitality as Wylie Duvall would succumb to dementia, unable to even run his own affairs."

Rhett felt his mother tense, and quickly intercepted the conversation. "Thanks for helping us out here, Charlie. As I explained on the phone, we need to get all the paperwork signed to remove Wylie from the accounts and officially add both me and my mother's names."

Charlie pointed them to a chair, moved behind his desk, and took a seat. "Well, as I told you, Grace is already on all the accounts. We have the paperwork ready to add Rhett in place of Wylie." He motioned to a clerk, who quickly delivered a file containing the documents into his hand.

He placed the file in the center of his desk and opened it, then he slid the papers across the desk and handed his mom a pen. "Grace, you sign right there." He pointed to a line with an "X" marked to the side.

She did as she was instructed and handed the pen to Rhett. He signed at the places designated and slipped the documents back to Charlie. "Could you run the balances for us in those accounts?" He made a mental note to set himself up on the online banking as soon as he got home.

"Sure thing. I will warn you, Wylie did come in last week and made a significant withdrawal. I wasn't here at that time, but I saw the transaction on my weekly report."

"A withdrawal?" Grace asked. Then, as if to assure herself, she quickly added, "Of course, it wasn't unusual for Wylie to access cash for various purposes."

Rhett frowned. "A big withdrawal?"

Charlie nodded. "I don't remember exactly, but it was a six-figure amount, from combined accounts."

"What?" Grace and Rhett exclaimed in unison.

"Why didn't you call me?" Grace demanded.

Charlie was quick to defend himself. "Why would I, Grace? I don't meddle in my customers' financial transactions. Until yesterday, none of us were aware there might be any issue with Wylie's mental abilities."

Rhett didn't need to peruse the accounts to know withdrawing that amount of cash would impact the oyster operation. "What about the payroll account?" he quickly asked. "What's in there?" Payday was the day after tomorrow.

Charlie shook his head. "Yeah, that's where most of the cash was when Wylie drew down the balance."

Before Rhett could let the information completely sink in, a woman appeared. She wore a red dress tailored to her silhouette and a strand of pearls at her neckline. As she drew closer, Rhett recognized Barbara Anthony.

Her coordinating red heels made a clacking noise against the shiny tiled floor as she moved to join them. "Oh, Grace. How awful! I just learned of Wylie's illness yesterday. You must be devastated." She turned her gaze upon Rhett. "All of you must be crushed."

Barbara Anthony was not his mother's favorite person. "Thank you, Barbara," she said.

"What can I do to help?" she asked, her voice dripping with exaggerated sympathy. Thoughtfulness wasn't exactly her hallmark. Just the opposite. Mayor Anthony and her son were cutthroat business operators who would sell their neighbor down the road for an increase in profit.

"Thank you, but we're good," Rhett replied. He still wasn't fond of the idea of Craig Anthony leaving Diane alone and pregnant back in high school. While he didn't yet know the entire story, he could only imagine the details, and they weren't likely pretty. He supposed the guy got a little credit for doing the right thing years later and stepping into a paternal role with Diane's teenaged daughter. Still, he'd just as soon keep both Craig and Mayor Anthony at a distance.

"Well, if you change your mind—just let me know." She leaned and gave his mother a little squeeze before turning for her office, her shoes continuing to make that annoying tapping sounds.

Rhett gathered his copy of the papers. "Thanks for everything, Charlie. I'll look into those balances and check to see just what Pop did with cash."

"If he remembers," his mother said, standing.

He didn't, of course. Which meant the entire family spent the entire next day scouring every nook and cranny, hoping to find a hidden envelope filled with bills. Unfortunately, their efforts turned up nothing.

From the online records, Rhett saw that Pop had taken out a little over $120,000, nearly the amount necessary to meet next week's payroll. It took some scrambling, but Rhett was able to cover the withdrawal by transferring from the general operating account and by drawing on their line-of-credit. They had cash to cover it if he cashed in some of the business certificates of deposit, but he hated to do that. Interest rates were up, and he disliked interrupting the income flow.

Rhett set out to make a long-term financial plan, one that would include the advice he'd given his dad over the past couple of years. Investment was key, cash flow the underpinning. Because of the low debt-to-income ratio the operation maintained, profit projections remained stable.

Satisfied they'd dodged a bullet, Rhett walked out to the mailbox to collect the mail. That's when the next surprise bomb detonated.

There, he found a plain white envelope addressed to his pop. Inside was a fully executed and notarized copy of a loan agreement. A line of credit for nearly a half-million dollars.

The lender? None other than Anthony Enterprises.

19

Rhett slammed the loan document onto Craig Anthony's desk. "Okay, Craig. So, I'll grant you the fact you were likely unaware that my dad suffered from dementia. Still, I'm a bit uncertain why my mother was left in the dark. In fact, I'm down right unsure why Pop allowed you to coerce him into a loan. Especially when he had the option of going through regular financial channels if he needed extra operating capital." Rhett set his jaw. *Or why Pop hadn't discussed anything of this with him.*

Craig held up open palms in protest. "Look, Rhett. I'm not the bad guy here. I simply made a loan to a trusted friend in the community. Someone with an excellent credit history and a reputation for being financially sound." He paused briefly. "Just for the record, I don't make a practice of sharing clients' private business information. At times not even with my mother."

Rhett could feel his blood pressure rise evidenced by the pulsating vein in his neck. "Let's just cut to the chase. Pop said you approached him. Said you told him expansion was a viable option for such a successful operation and that you knew he'd need funds to make that happen. You told him the loan instrument would not be recorded, and therefore wouldn't affect his credit rating. That a line of credit would place instant cash in his hands any time needed."

Craig looked at him patiently. "Wylie might have said all those things, but—well, I'm not sure his memory can be counted on to be entirely accurate."

"That's really convenient for you, isn't it? Did you know? Were you suspicious about my dad's mental health?" Rhett curled his fists tightly, trying to keep from losing his patience. This character was the same as he'd always been—a ruthless jerk who grabbed at any opportunity to make a buck, no matter who or what situation he exploited.

"What?" Craig stood from his desk. "No, of course, I had no idea about your dad."

Craig was the same snake he'd always been, abusing friends, family, and anyone in need. If anyone doubted that, they could just ask Cam and Allie.

Craig had made an unsuccessful attempt to maneuver *Reel Chances* away from Allie and add the fishing vessel to his own fleet. His mother charged the Hendersons more interest for their car loan than any standard bank would have charged them, even with their unsteady credit rating. His mother, the mayor, appointed her son to the Pacific Bay Community Board, and miraculously, the extra lot owned by the library was deeded to Anthony Enterprises for less than market value.

And why was it that no one ever ran against Mayor Anthony? Rhett could only dare to guess after learning of veiled threats to pull in loans from teetering businesses and evict renters from the properties Craig and his mother owned. They had influence, and they used it for their purposes. No matter the cost to others.

Never mind the history between Craig and Diane. What kind of dude gets a girl pregnant and never steps up to his responsibilities until years later?

Rhett shook his head. He didn't like any of it, but the other situations were none of his business. Pop and the oyster farm, now *that* was his business and he planned to rectify everything today.

He took a deep breath. "Look, Craig. I'm canceling the loan."

"Are you sure you want to do that?" Craig told him. "Early termination immediately invokes provision twelve."

"Surely, you don't intend to enforce the prepayment penalty? I mean, especially given the circumstances."

Craig leaned back in his office chair, steepled his fingers. "Business is business."

"Fine!" Knowing the operating account had little cash, Rhett pulled his personal checkbook from his back pocket. "How much?"

When Craig quoted a figure, Rhett nearly choked. He angrily scribbled out the amount and tossed the check across the desk. "I don't necessarily believe in karma. But if I did, I sure wouldn't be sorry to see it come back to bite you."

Craig stood and laughed as he extended a hand across the desk. "Oh, c'mon. I was only trying to do your dad a favor. It didn't work out, but there's no reason to appoint any animosity to the deal. Friends?"

Rhett left his hand hanging. Instead, he slid a document out of his briefcase and onto the desk. "Sign at the bottom. It's a full loan satisfaction stating the loan is rescinded."

Craig pulled his Mont Blanc pen from its holder and signed. "There."

Out in the car, Rhett tossed his briefcase onto the seat next to him and rolled his window up against the storm blowing in from the west.

He was nearly home when his phone rang. It was Diane.

"Hey, what's up?" he asked as he drove past the marina, trying to force the stress from his voice.

"Hi, Rhett," she said. "Are you okay? You sound...mad."

He had to smile. She was pretty intuitive. He'd had years of practice working the anger from his voice with clients. "I'm—well, I'm better now."

"Oh, good. I wanted to call and check in with you. I was a little worried after yesterday and was anxious to hear how things went when you got Wylie home."

Rhett couldn't believe how much he appreciated hearing from her. "That's really thoughtful. I'm sorry. I should have called you."

"No, no," she assured him. "You had a lot on your plate. But, how is he—your dad?"

Rhett told her his father was fine, that the whole family was fine. "It's going to take a little time to assimilate to this new thing in our lives. Pop's always been such a strong figure in our family. He's the glue that held us together. These changes—well, they're not easy." He told her what they'd discovered upon going to the bank, and what they'd discovered later in the envelope.

"Oh, I'm so sorry. That must be heartbreaking watching your dad become someone else. Craig can be such a royal rear-end. Can't something be done, legally?"

"With everything else, I don't need a court battle looming over a few thousand dollars. No, I just have to write the prepay penalty off."

"Sounds like you're staying just ahead of the fire."

Diane's choice of words made Rhett chuckle. "Yeah, feels like. Hopefully, we've gotten ahead of this thing, and there will be no more surprises." But Rhett knew that with Pop's diagnosis, there could be plenty more surprises to come. At least the business was safe now.

"Look," she told him. "Maybe you're far too busy...or you have more pressing matters to attend to, but I'd like to do something nice for you. Any chance you'd like to meet me out on

Whaler's Point for a picnic? Mom says the grays have just started to migrate."

"A picnic?"

"Yeah. You don't have to worry about a thing. I'll pack a basket and a blanket. It's—well, it's what friends are for."

The term hung there, each of them weighing the meaning, before Rhett spoke up. "I'd like that."

"Great! Then, is tomorrow good?"

"Tomorrow's great." They set a time before hanging up.

Rhett pocketed his phone and grinned. For a day that started out so crappy, events sure had a way of turning around.

Upon returning home, Rhett wandered down to the processing shed, hoping to find Pop. His dad immediately cornered him. "Son, got a minute?"

"Sure, Pop. What do you need?"

His father frowned and motioned him outside where they could talk without their voices having to compete for air space over the grinding engines in the conveyors and tumblers. "Your mom tells me you and she went to the bank this morning."

Rhett dropped his gaze to the cement floor. "Yeah, we did," he admitted.

His pop placed a hand on his shoulder and guided him past large metal shucking tables and down the wooden pier to the pilings at the end. He rubbed at his chin while looking out over the familiar scene—the bay that stretched for several miles. The large pines lining the bank on the distant shoreline. He scanned the acres filled with man-made reefs making up the habitat for the oysters until they grew to be market size and ready for harvest.

Rhett's dad was as much a part of this landscape as any mud flat or estuary filled with brackish water.

"You took me off the accounts," his father finally stated.

A heavy pause hung in the foggy air. "Yeah, Pop. I had to. As much as I hate it, we had no choice but to make some changes. Especially after yesterday. Pop, you scared us."

His father slowly nodded, his expression hard to read. "Well, there's only one thing left to say then." He folded his arms across his chest. "It's time for you to go home."

20

Rhett eased his car off the highway onto the pullout at Whaler's Point and pulled to a stop. He cut the engine and took a deep breath. After all the events of this week, he really needed this and had looked forward to spending time with Diane since receiving her call.

He grabbed the bottle of sparkling cider and the plastic stemmed glasses from the seat and stepped from his new SUV. He spotted Diane sitting on a blanket, perched on a grassy knoll overlooking the ocean.

Rhett waved and carefully stepped across a rock cropping as he made his way toward her.

"Hey," she called out when he neared. "New car?"

"Yeah, the rental was no longer cost-effective. So, I made a quick run to Eugene and bought this one."

"Well, it's nice," she said, patting the blanket next to her. "I like the color."

He settled down in the spot where she'd indicated and held up the bottle. "Hope you like red," he bantered. "I stopped by Susan Wilson's shop down on Highway 101, and she promised it's a good one."

"Looks really good," she told him, smiling. "I'm normally a Dr Pepper kind-of-girl. This will be a real treat." She opened her picnic basket while he poured their drinks. "I hope you like what I fixed for lunch—well, what Mother fixed. When she heard we were going to come out here to try to spot some whales, she insisted on pulling together some sandwiches. Ham and gruyere cheese, I believe."

"Looks delicious," he said, taking one from her hand. He nodded toward the ocean. "Have you spotted any yet?"

Diane nodded with enthusiasm. "Four, so far. One even breached clear out of the water."

They ate in silence for several moments, taking in the magnificent views. Suddenly, Diane let her sandwich drop to the napkin in her lap. She pointed. "There, see? Another one spouting."

His gaze followed where she pointed. "Yeah, I see it. Wow." He shook his head. "That never gets old."

"No, it doesn't," she agreed. Then she turned to him. "So, how are you? Yesterday...well, that was pretty big."

He set his sandwich down as well and grabbed for his glass. He swirled the rose-colored liquid, watching bubbles drift to the top. "Yeah, I've had better days," he admitted. "I guess I thought we'd have more time. I mean, I know the internet warned that all cases differ, even Dr. Michaels explained that symptoms build at various paces." He swallowed. "I just—well, I thought we'd be one of the lucky families, and Pop's decline would progress very slowly."

Her face filled with sympathy. She reached and patted his leg. "I get it. There's nothing much harder than saying goodbye to a parent, no matter the means. I remember when we lost Dad all those years ago, it felt like the entire world had imploded underneath my feet. I was in an emotional freefall for —well, for some time." She offered a faraway smile. "I still miss him."

"I think I took a lot of things for granted."

"What do you mean?" she asked.

Rhett looked down at cider. "Deep down, I assumed Pop would always be here, that I could pick up the phone and talk to him at any given moment. I believed the memories we share would remain constant. Lewy's dementia is a slow death that cuts at your heart like being stabbed by a thousand needles." He told her about his father's reaction to taking him off the accounts and the hurtful thing he'd said as a result.

"I'm so sorry," she said. "Even knowing that's the disease talking, that had to have stung."

Rhett let his gaze drift past her to the ocean's surface stretching out as far as the eye could see. "Had I known what was ahead, maybe I would have made different choices with my life."

"You mean you might have remained in Pacific Bay and near your family?"

He had a strange reaction to how easily she read him. "That, among other things."

She gave him another of those earnest looks, seeming to let his comment settle a bit. "Well, all I've got to say is that you're looking at someone who used to wear the title *Queen of Regret*. Take it from me, looking behind and wishing you'd made different choices serves no value. You can't live in the past, Rhett. And, there's no way to predict what the future really holds. The only wise thing to do is to live in the moment, wring every drop of joy out of the present."

He knew she was right. She not only wore an expression that made him feel he was free to tell her anything, there was something decidedly calming about being in her presence. Sure, she was beautiful. In fact, Diane was a natural beauty. Long strands of hair swept her shoulders as the wind blew across her face and body, ruffling her shirt and the corners of the checkered blanket. When the breeze changed direction and hit him straight on, he could smell a light fragrance—or maybe it was her shampoo? He didn't know, but he found himself leaning closer to catch another whiff.

He'd seen pictures of her on the internet (yes, he'd looked) and she was different back when she lived in California. No doubt, her hair, face and nails were professionally fixed up. She looked a lot like the girls he'd dated back in Chicago. He'd hate to see some of their beauty bills. Looking like a million bucks was expensive. He had a client who made a fortune in the early years of Botox injections.

She was different now. It was as if she no longer needed to impress anyone. The confidence of living in her own skin was far more intoxicating than pouty-enhanced lips or perfect makeup and hair.

Rhett liked how Diane's hair felt—soft like a silk and colored a dozen shades of blonde. He'd noticed that the other night when he'd been bold enough to brush that kiss against her ear, meant to be a friendly notion. Admittedly, it'd been far more. He'd like to repeat the experience right now, and—

"Rhett?"

"Huh? Oh, sorry."

She smiled at him. "Where'd you go?"

He swiftly shook his head. "Nowhere. Just thinking." He let his gaze meet hers. "About what you said," he added. He lifted his glass to his lips and tossed back the remaining cider.

"Enough about me," he said, putting his empty glass down. "I want to know more about you. Tell me about your daughter."

That brought a wide smile to her face. "She's beautiful," she told him. "And sassy. Smart, too." She bit lightly at her bottom lip before adding, "I simply make no bones about the fact I adore her."

"I hear she's taken up with Pastor Riggin's kid."

"Oh, I don't know about *taken up*, but they are good friends."

Rhett reached for the bottle. "Nothing wrong with being good friends." He grinned at her while refilling his glass, then held up the bottle to her. "Ready for some more?"

"Love some," she said, and gathered her hair over one shoulder. She held out her glass, and he filled it to the top.

Wow, he'd love nothing more than to run his fingers through her hair. Friends, or no, she was pulling at him. Surely, she could see it in his eyes. He'd have to get hold of himself, or risk messing this up.

"When I left Pacific Bay all those years back, I was a mess. My self-esteem was in the toilet. I couldn't believe I'd let myself believe Craig Anthony actually had feelings for me. Or that I'd taken my guard down and—well, you know."

Rhett shrugged. "His loss." He wondered if Craig now realized what he'd let go. Did he have any regrets?

"Anyway, my daughter was the one thing that proved I could do something right. Sadly, over the course of time, my insecurities continued to play out, and I let her down, too. She had every right to be an angry teenager."

"Mom tells me she's a really sweet little gal. And she's is a good judge of character."

Diane grinned and stretched her legs out on the blanket. "That's good to hear. And, yes, she is now. We've both had a lot of work to do on ourselves. Seems the healthier I got, the more it rubbed off on Stacey. Of course, my mother influenced the matter, as well." She explained the strained relationship she'd had with her mother, how much she'd resented her mom's attempts to mold her early choices. "I felt like she was judging me. The reality was, I was judging myself and knew I came up far short of my own expectations. Every time another of my marriages failed, the disappointment cemented the notion I was nothing more than a screw-up."

Before he could respond, she held up an open hand to stop him. "Oh, I know. But it's the truth. My drinking only made things worse." Her face broke into a weak smile. "Before you throw me a pity party, I no longer believe any of those lies. In fact, I really like who I am. I like my life."

"That's what it is," he said, staring at her.

"What?"

"That something about you." He couldn't help himself. He reached and lightly touched her bare arm.

"Look!" She pointed.

He diverted his attention to the vast ocean in time to see a gigantic gray whale lift from the water and come crashing down. The motion sent a massive spray of water in all directions, only yards from shore. The sight nearly took his breath away.

He grabbed for the binoculars he'd packed, offered them to her.

She took them and brought them to her face. While she was searching the water's surface for another whale, Rhett took the opportunity to fully appreciate the woman sitting next to him. Never had he shared this kind of intimacy—talked so openly about such private matters. He found himself wanting to spill even the things he'd so carefully hidden—his fear, his own feelings of falling short in a world that expected a real man to have it all together.

For all his accomplishments, he longed for someone to share those successes with. Yet, until now, he'd barely understood that kind of longing. Truth was, he wanted what his mom and dad had built, a relationship that would get a couple through anything. Even the worst. Even dementia. But it had never occurred to him that bonds like that do not just happen. They take work, commitment, time. Until now, he hadn't been ready to devote any of those things to a relationship because all of his energy went into work.

She dropped the binoculars from her face and turned to him. "Mom says whales do that as a form of communication."

Her eyes glistened with excitement. "Can you even imagine what it sounds like under the water when those huge mammals slap the surface like that?"

Their gazes met and held.

They stayed like that for several seconds before Rhett let out a light cough. "Hey, I don't know what you guys are doing for Thanksgiving next week, but would you consider joining us for dinner out at Mom's? I know she'd love to have all of you."

Diane paused, thought about his offer. She lifted those large dark eyes to his. "Well, Mom and Grace are good friends. I'm sure my mother would love that." She let her fingers drift to his. "Truthfully, I would, too."

He felt an immediate smile come to his lips. Not only was she beautiful, she was amazing.

Rhett knew at that moment that despite his promise to the contrary—he considered Diane much, much more than simply a friend. She was kind and sensitive. Smart and hardworking. She didn't take herself too seriously, or let him get too down on himself. Even when he deserved a knock —or two.

It seemed he could tell her anything and never feel judgment. Just the opposite. She helped him shed the hurts, the worry. She gave him the ability to grasp the upside to the hard situations he faced.

It was difficult to fully explain, but somehow when he was with Diane, he felt *known*. He didn't need to perform, fix, or impress. He could simply be himself.

Truth was, she was everything he'd always wanted in a long-term relationship. In fact, Diane Jeffers might be the kind of woman he could spend the rest of his life with.

The thought startled him. Scared him.

Rhett had never dared to feel that way about any woman. Surely, it was too early to move that fast. Didn't this kind of thing take time? He barely knew her, and yet he felt like he'd known her forever. Did he have the guts to embrace this thing? To see where it all might lead?

What if she never felt the same and really was determined to stay out of another relationship?

What if he was setting himself up for a broken heart?

"Rhett?"

Her voice interrupted his thoughts. He swallowed, hard. "Sorry. I was lost in thought again. I really need to stop doing that." He ran a hand through his hair.

She studied his face. "Easy to do out here." She gave him a moment before leaning back on outstretched arms. "I asked if we could bring anything?"

"Huh? Oh, I—I'm not sure, really. I'll have Mom reach out to your mother and they can figure it all out."

Diane nodded. "That's a good plan. I'm sure the two of them can dream up something great, in terms of a feast." She gave him a sidelong look. "It's—well, I'm looking forward to it," she told him, a bit breathless.

He looked into those dark, liquid eyes for a long moment before making a bold and risky decision. He hadn't climbed to the top of the financial world by holding back. He moved closer, rubbed a knuckle down her cheek. "Diane, let's quit talking about turkey and focus on what I suspect we're both feeling here."

"I'm not sure I'm ready to take that chance," she told him, pulling back slightly. "I owe it to Stacey, and to myself, not to adhere to another man so soon. In fact, I need to learn to be on my own, to not need that other side of the bed filled. Know what I mean?"

He heard the words. Yet her eyes sent a different message.

"I understand," he said, letting his hand drop. "I don't blame you, given your history and all the men who have let you down. I'm not those men."

She bit at the inside of her cheek. "I believe that. I do. It's not your fault that you're stuck with this. I'm so sorry, but I don't think I can—"

"Diane, we're in no hurry. We'll take all the time you need," he told her. "I can't fix your past. I don't know what the future holds. I do know that, eventually, I want to be more than just your friend. I think that's what you want, too. At least, I hope so." He gave her hand a squeeze. "Let's just stay in the present and wring every bit of joy this life has to offer. For now, we don't have to go any further than that."

The corners of her lips turned up in a slight smile as she realized he'd turned her own words back on her. She let out a deep sigh. "Okay," she said. "I suppose I can do that."

"You'll call the shots, Diane. We won't move any faster than what makes you feel comfortable. We're no longer kids." He took her hand and brought it to his mouth, brushed his lips against her soft skin, wishing it was her mouth he was kissing. "We have all the time in the world."

She looked skeptical. "That's not entirely true," she argued. "You're on sabbatical. Even if your work break is long-term, you'll be going back to Chicago, eventually."

"I'm not sure that's so," he admitted. "There are a lot of reasons to stay and make Pacific Bay my home again." The notion seemed to come out of nowhere. Yet, if he were honest, he'd been considering moving back for a while now. After resigning his position at the equity firm, he'd placed everything he owned in storage, had sold his car in Chicago and bought a new one here. There was no doubt he needed to stay. He hadn't considered making the move permanent, but now that he thought about it, he knew moving back was what he wanted.

Especially now.

He looked out at the ocean. Then met her eyes and found warmth there, saw her smile at the news he might be remaining in Pacific Bay.

"You're staying?"

Rhett nodded. "I need to be with my family as we travel this journey with Pop. Even after, I want to be here to watch over my mom, sister and brother. I'm the oldest. I have responsibilities."

Even more, he had to admit there was a hole inside that was beginning to fill again. Truth was, his heart was making its way back home. The woman sitting next to him was a big part of that. He told her so. "I'm not one to mince words. Especially when there's so much at stake. So, let me be clear. Someday, I'm going to kiss you, Diane. It may not be time yet, maybe not even soon—but someday." He laughed out loud in spite of himself.

That was a promise he intended to keep.

21

Ever since Rhett could remember, Thanksgiving at his mom's house had been filled with tradition. His mother always bought the biggest turkey she could find, leaving it in the store cooler to thaw several days before the big holiday. She and his sister made multiple trips to the market, loading up on all the ingredients they'd need for the Duvall feast.

His mother made her special sage dressing with dried bread crumbs of her own making. "The store-bought kind just isn't as good," she'd explained more often than Rhett could accurately recall. She also made another with oysters. Those who sat around her table raved about it, saying it was the best they'd ever eaten. Pop was known to eat three helpings.

She prepared several kinds of side dishes. His personal favorite was some kind of green gelatin she whipped with dried pistachio pudding mix, crushed pineapple and whipped cream. Then, she added chopped pistachio nuts. He also looked forward to her shrimp cocktail with chopped celery and bay shrimp stirred into cocktail sauce.

His sister was the pie master and spent the week before

their big dinner preparing nearly a dozen different kinds. Pumpkin, of course, but she also had marionberry and pecan made with locally grown berries and nuts. She also used locally grown apples for a pie that could easily grace the cover of any food magazine.

His personal contribution was the mashed potatoes. He knew just the right quantity of crème to add to the boiled russets while mashing. The end result? A massive bowl of mouth-watering spuds that were so creamy, it would bring tears to your eyes. Especially when doused with his mom's turkey gravy.

This year, he had more to look forward to beyond the delicious fare that would be spread across their holiday table. This year, Diane would be joining them, along with her mother and daughter. Upon the suggestion of his mom, an invitation had also been extended to Pastor Riggin and his son, Nolan. That would make Diane's daughter happy.

Since their afternoon together late last week, he could barely get Diane out of his mind. He went to bed thinking about all they had said that day and woke up thinking about all he still wanted to say to her. He brushed his teeth, remembering how she looked. And those smiles...ah, her smile could lift him from deep places. She brought a lightness to his soul. He couldn't wait to see her again. He texted her on several occasions to tell her so.

Goodness, he felt like a schoolboy with a crush on the prettiest girl in class.

Even Ben and Cam noticed when he'd met them yesterday for a quick beer down at the Sea Star Tavern.

"Okay, that's the third time you've brought up Diane Jeffers's name in less than fifteen minutes. What's up with that?" Ben leaned and removed his wallet from his pocket. He opened it and slipped out his credit card, then handed it off to Axel. "This round is on me." He turned his attention back to the table. "I mean, you got the hots for her or something?"

When Rhett didn't deny the assertion immediately, Cam's eyebrows shot up. "Hey, what gives? You holding out on your old buddies?" He slapped Rhett on the back. "Time to come clean, bro."

Rhett shook his head, reached for his beer. "It's nothing like that."

"Sure. And that's the only brew you're going to drink this week." Cam laughed.

"Rumor has it, she might feel the same way about you," Ben confided.

Rhett's eyebrows drew together. "Why? What did you hear?"

Ben took a long draw off his beer. He set the bottle back on the table. "Well, Olivia tells me she's mentioned your name a few times. Olivia thinks you two would make a cute couple, and she told Diane that."

Cam chuckled. "Allie thinks so, too."

Rhett couldn't believe these two. The town gossips had nothing on these guys sitting across from him, cackling like old women.

Rhett crossed his bedroom, buttoning his shirt. He looked out the window at the fog building across the bay.

Let them have their fun, he thought. Fact was, they weren't that far off nailing the truth. It delighted him to know Diane's good friends were assessing the situation as well and were perhaps nudging her in his direction.

He smiled. It was true. Despite the passing years, in many ways, they were all still back in high school.

Downstairs, his mom and sister were busy in a flurry of activity. "Shoo," his mother said, waving him away as he approached. "Get your coffee and head out. We've got a lot to do."

His sister took pity. "There's a box of donuts next to the pot."

He gave her a grateful look. "Thanks. I'm glad I don't have to go hungry."

His mother huffed. "No one is going hungry today. I guarantee it."

He leaned and kissed her cheek, risking a slap of her towel on his backside. Then he carried his mug of coffee and donut out the back door.

"Don't forget to wear a jacket," his mother called out. "Don't want you getting sick."

He laughed to himself, moved back inside, and slipped a light coat from the hooks just inside the back door. "Got it," he called back.

Rhett took a bite of donut and made his way to the dock. There were only three days a year when Pop shut down operations—Thanksgiving, Christmas, and Easter. He believed the men needed to be with their families on these special holidays.

The processing shed was quiet as Rhett strode past the wash pumps, the tumblers, and the shiny metal sorting tables. The air smelled faintly of sea algae and brine, of the tang of oysters. While others might lift their nostrils in disgust, he loved the smell. Rhett smiled, remembering Pop often claimed it was the smell of money.

He wandered through the long shed to the other end where an open sliding door led to the moorings and the long wooden pier where Pop and Jared stood looking out over the channel lined with man-made reefs holding clumps of growing oysters.

"We're getting another shipment of spat next week, Pop." Jared took a sip from his mug. "From that new company in Canada we used last summer."

Pop nodded with approval. "That crop had deep cups, meaty oysters."

Rhett joined them. "Hey, you two."

Jared tossed the remaining liquid from his nearly empty coffee mug out over the water. "Hey, bro. We were just chatting business." He smiled at his brother as if to say Pop was having a good day. He was engaged and his memory clear.

Funny how the entire family had learned to communicate in looks, grunts, and sighs.

Rhett squeezed his dad's shoulder. "Gonna be a good harvest, you think?"

Pop rubbed at his chin. "Might be the best one in years," he claimed. "God's been good to us." He pointed to the reefs. "Those babies are growing at a rate I haven't seen in a while. Something in the water."

Wylie glanced between his boys. "I have a secret," he said.

Both Rhett and Jared stiffened. They shared a worried look. "Yeah, what's that?" Rhett asked, hoping they weren't about to face another surprise that would need dealt with.

"I'm going to take your mother on a cruise to Alaska," he announced. "She's begged me to go for years. Never could get away." Wylie let his gaze drift across the channel where tips of tall ponderosa pines peeked above the fog bank. "Well, now I have you two. You have proven you are more than capable of holding down this operation for a short time. And, besides—" Pop paused. "Well, we all know time's short. If I don't take her now, I might never have the opportunity."

Jared blinked away sudden tears. "I think that's a great idea, Pop."

Rhett found himself wanting to argue. There were many reasons a trip like that might not be advisable given Pop's condition. Could his mom handle things if Pop took a turn for the worse? Still, he couldn't bring himself to try and convince his father not to go on the excursion. If it came to that, Jared or he could drop everything and go get them. That was the way life was now. He took nothing for granted.

Less than a few months ago, Rhett left Chicago on what he

thought was a short vacation. His plan was to join in celebrating his father's birthday, then he was going to return home and close the big Markowitz deal.

Look how that had turned out.

He still hadn't told his family of his plans to move back. There was time for all that. Right now, he simply focused on staying in the present. Diane taught him that.

The three men stood at the end of the pier, chatting about everything, and nothing at all. Seemed time was a gift these days, and none of them were in a hurry to end their conversation. Especially when it meant going back to the house and encountering busy women.

Jared rubbed the back of his neck. "So, Mom tells us you asked Diane Jeffers and her family to join us for dinner."

Pop warmed at that. He nodded. "Good move, son. Ellen Jeffers is a good woman. She raised a good daughter. Diane certainly had her share of detours, but that gal is a fine example of what it means to turn your life around." He looked at Jared as if to punctuate his sentence. "Seems there's a lot of that going around these days."

Perhaps Rhett should have cleared the air, clarified just what their relationship was—and wasn't. Yet, it didn't really seem all that important. Let them think what they would. If he had his way, the relationship would turn to one far more intimate. Sooner rather than later would satisfy him in that regard.

"Well, hey, I need to go take a shower and get this stink off me," Jared said, turning to walk back to the house.

"Sure that's possible, bro?" Rhett teased.

Jared laughed and waved off his comment. "See you up at the house." He sauntered away, carrying his empty coffee mug in one hand with his other deep inside his jeans pocket.

Rhett decided to take the opportunity to tell his dad about his recent decision. "Pop?"

"Yeah, son?"

"I've decided to move home."

Before he could explain his reasoning, his father whipped around with a big scowl. "Oh, I was afraid of that." His pop ran his hand over his balding head. "Moving home to take care of all of us isn't a good idea. In fact, it's a very bad idea."

Rhett suddenly felt like a scolded kid. He shrugged. "My decision makes sense for a lot of reasons. Granted, you do all need my help—well, given your diagnosis. But, then—"

"Hogwash!" his dad barked. "That's just why your mom and I kept all this from you initially. We knew you'd do something stupid and topple your own life, your career. You'd make some pious, sanctimonious sacrifice for the good of the family at a huge cost to you personally. No, son." Wylie shook his head. "I won't let you do it."

"It's already done, Pop," Rhett told him. He altered the truth a bit and explained how his job had consumed everything he had to give, suggested it was his decision to leave the firm. It was, of course. He was also given a mighty hefty shove toward the door. "My work wasn't healthy, Pop. I slaved away nearly twenty-four seven. I went through two relationships. I didn't have any friends. Never saw any of you more than once a year, if that. My bank account was growing, but my soul was shrinking." He looked his pop in the eyes. "Yes, the timing with your Lewy's coincided and was the thing that pushed me over the cliff, but believe me—it really was only a matter of time before I eventually woke up and made a change." Rhett wasn't sure he believed that himself, but the story was close to the truth and sounded convincing. "It's the right thing for me to do, on many counts."

Rhett let his gaze meet his Pop's.

He'd heard it said before that age was a cruel mistress, or was that time? He couldn't quite recall. He hadn't fully understood the meaning back then, but now the cruelty of his pop's dementia and how it seemed to be transforming his dad before his very eyes was sadly becoming apparent. Rhett couldn't help but notice his pop's once purposeful stride was now replaced with an unbalanced amble. Liver spots crept over the backs of his hands and his confident eyes were often now filled with doubt—or was that fear?

Pop had been spry and mentally alert, then the downhill slide came as rapidly as a winter wave crashing onshore. It had knocked all of them to their knees at some level.

Pop cleared his throat. "Listen, Rhett. I'm proud of you, son. I don't think I've ever really told you that. I should have." Pop fought to keep his lip from quivering. "And, I'm sorry."

"Sorry, Pop?"

"For leaving you like this. For leaving all of you."

22

"Pass the gravy," Rhett's little nephew demanded, reaching across his plate for the bowl.

"Hey, buddy. Manners," Leila scolded. "And wait your turn."

The little guy sunk back in his chair, sporting a forlorn look. "But Dad's taking it all."

His grandmother chuckled. "Don't worry, Billy. There's plenty more in the kitchen."

Grace had been up since well before dawn. She'd stuffed an enormous turkey and placed the holiday bird in the oven before anyone else in the house had risen. In her mind, holidays were meant to be special, especially Thanksgiving. Despite Wylie's diagnosis, they all had much to be thankful for.

Moments earlier, her eyes had been filled with tears as Wylie stood to offer the blessing. When he stumbled over finding words, he got extremely frustrated and dropped his linen napkin to the table. "Oh, never mind. Jared, you do it."

Everyone around the table nervously glanced at each other as Jared slowly nodded. He scraped his chair back against the dining room floor and stood. Those at the table took their cue and bowed their heads again.

"Father, thank you for the pleasure of gathering around this table with beloved family and friends. We give thanks for this food prepared by loving hands. We give thanks for life, the freedom to enjoy each and every day, and all the blessings you've provided. Give us hearts filled with appreciation, and don't let us take any of your blessings for granted. As we eat today, we pray for health and strength to carry on and live as you would have us." He paused, swallowed the emotion building. "Amen."

A hardy "amen" was cited from those sitting around the table.

Rhett and Jared's eyes met. Rhett gave a slight nod of approval and Jared sat.

"That was a wonderful prayer," Pastor Riggin said. "Heartfelt and spot on."

"I agree," Grace said, looking proud. She stood and took the gravy bowl in her hands. "Keep eating. I'll be right back."

"Could you get us some more of those rolls?" Wes asked as he scooped a large mound of dressing and plopped it on his plate next to the generous slices of turkey.

Little Levi folded his arms and let his back fall against his chair. "I don't like this stuff. Can I just have punkin' pie?"

Leila rolled her eyes. "Sorry, everyone." She turned to her youngest son. "Honey, you have to eat some of this first. Otherwise, how will you grow big like your Papa and Daddy?"

"But I don't like it!" he whined.

Wes lifted his eyebrows and shrugged. "I'll eat whatever he doesn't."

How that man didn't gain a ton of weight, Rhett didn't know. His brother-in-law consumed enough for three men his size.

Ellen Jeffers tucked her napkin on her lap. "Grace, all this looks delicious. We appreciate this invite so much. Truly a wonderful thing, celebrating with all of you."

Diane nodded in agreement. "Yes, we are so tickled to be here. Thank you." She lightly nudged her daughter, who was busy gazing at Nolan.

"Uh, yeah," Stacey offered. "Really nice of you, Mrs. Duvall."

Nolan clapped his hands together. "I can't wait to try that sweet potato casserole."

As was tradition, Rhett's mom had whipped the sweet potatoes with brown sugar and then mounded the top with toasted marshmallows. It was a favorite every year.

As was also tradition, everyone ate until stuffed. And then, out came the desserts. By the time Rhett pushed back from the table, his stomach actually hurt.

The table was cleared, dishes cleaned and put away. Everyone helped, even the youngsters. "You all eat, you all help clean," Grace often said. When the kitchen chores were finished, the men retired in the den to watch football while the women poured cups of coffee and gathered around the table to chat.

Early in the fourth quarter, the Cleveland Browns had pulled sufficiently ahead that a win was assured. Rhett could stand it no more. He lifted from his spot on the sofa and wandered into the kitchen where the women were now discussing upcoming Christmas plans.

The outdoor nativity would have to be put up on the church lawn, complete with donkeys from out at Scott BeVier's tiny farm. Decorations would be erected all over town, with real pine garlands strung over the windows of the retail shops. Pots filled with fall chrysanthemums, the bloom edges now turning brown, would be replaced with bright red poinsettias.

Wylie often played Santa down at the town gazebo. This year, his condition would force changes. Despite his protests to the contrary, Mayor Anthony strongly suggested that her son would make the ideal replacement. Few others in town agreed with her choice and suggested they open up nominations and vote. Even so, Rhett was putting his money on Craig Anthony ending up the winner of that contest. Mayor Anthony seldom lost a campaign.

Diane looked up and their eyes met. Rhett tilted his head toward the door. She smiled and pushed her chair back. "I think I'm going to take a walk," she said.

The others at the table glanced between Rhett and Diane, then at each other. Grace's face broke into a wide smile. "Shoo, go! Enjoy yourselves."

Ellen waved them toward the door. "I agree. Go!"

The reluctant couple faced three expectant faces. Big eyes. Wide grins.

Embarrassed by the attention, Rhett grabbed Diane's jacket and held it for her as she slipped her arms inside the sleeves. "We won't be long," he promised.

"No hurry," Leila told them. She, too, sported a huge grin.

As soon as they were outside, Diane shook her head. "I think our family believes this is a little more than we intend."

"What? You mean our *friendship*?" he teased.

She gave his shoulder a playful nudge. "You know what I mean. They are pushing far ahead of what is going on between us. Frankly, I'm surprised my mother is doing that, given my history."

Rhett grinned. "She likes me."

They wandered toward the far end of the bay. "Oh, you think so, huh?"

Rhett gave an exaggerated shrug. "What can I say? I'm very likeable. Some say I have all the qualities of great boyfriend material."

"Boyfriend?" Diane laughed. "What are we—back in high school?"

They made their way down the path that led along the water's edge. "Speaking of boyfriends, looks like that Nolan kid is pretty smitten with your daughter," Rhett mentioned as he bent and picked up a tiny stone and tossed it onto the water's surface. The motion created a ripple, which circled the water, spreading slowly. "He could barely pull his eyes from her all through dinner."

Diane let out a sigh. "Yeah, you're probably right. She's at that age. That scares me," she admitted.

"What? Seems to me she couldn't find anyone better than the pastor's kid. He seems polite and respectful." Rhett tossed another rock. "Can't ask for much more than that."

Diane found a large rock, brushed it off and sat. "I know you're right. I'm just not ready for that stage in her life. I mean, I know she's got a good head on her shoulders. I think the world of Nolan Riggin. He is a good boy. I know that. It's just..." She let her voice drift off.

Rhett watched a seagull swoop and land on a wooden piling. "So, what are you really afraid of?"

"Well, a lot of things," she quickly insisted. "First, I'm scared Stacey will follow in my footsteps. Relationships are not to be entered into lightly. Missteps have consequences."

Rhett turned and gazed at the woman beside him, taking in how pretty she looked in the sweater and how great her legs looked in those knee-high leather boots. "Are we still talking about your daughter?"

His question was met with momentary silence. Finally, Diane met his gaze. "Maybe not," she admitted. She picked up a twig and drew in the wet sand at her feet. "I'm working on all this."

"In group?" he asked.

She nodded.

"With Jared?" Rhett didn't know why he added that. He knew instantly from the look on her face that he'd crossed a boundary. No one in Alcoholics Anonymous broke confidences and shared what they talked about in meetings. "Sorry, I just—"

"It seems you two are making progress," she said, changing the subject.

"I took your advice. You were right," he admitted. "Bitterness can eat you up inside. I'm trying really hard to see things from Jared's perspective. I see now that he has changed. He's different, and I'm proud of him."

Diane beamed. "That's so good to hear, Rhett. Truly." She tossed the twig aside. "Feels good, doesn't it? I mean, leaving the junk behind and moving on." She stopped talking.

"Yes, it does feel good," Rhett said cautiously, wondering if she'd realized what she'd said.

She broke her gaze and looked across the water. "I suppose you think I need to follow my own advice."

Rhett was smart enough to stay quiet on that point. Instead, he decided to hear her out.

"I'm so scared," she admitted. "My life is so good, right now. I don't want to mess this up."

Rhett lifted his eyebrow. "You think taking our relationship a step further would mess your life up?"

"No—yes, I mean—I don't know," she said, distracted by some deep thought. "Mom tells me you were engaged once. Tell me about your fiancée."

"My fiancée?"

"Yes, tell me about her." Her expression turned serious. "What happened? Why did you end things?"

Rhett swallowed. What was there to say? He'd been stupid...and selfish. Diane wasn't the only one to make mistakes in the romance department. And he told her so.

"Actually, she broke off the engagement."

Rhett hadn't thought about Cherie for a long time. His mind drifted back to those early days right after he'd moved to

Chicago. Things were tight then. He worked around the clock, especially since most of his income was commission-based. In addition to managing the accounts assigned to him, he manned the order desk at night. And sleep? He had barely known he meaning of the word. The days were long, the nights short, the sales efforts intense.

So when he was invited to an after-hours office party, his first inclination was to say no. Remembering advice he'd received at an earlier Chicago Economic Outlook luncheon, he decided to push aside his reservations and take advantage of an opportunity to network. "The lone wolf howls to no one," warned his mentor.

It was there at that party, held at the prestigious Forest Glen Country Club, that he met the woman who would steal his heart for the first time.

Cherie Nicholson Wallace was the daughter of a man who'd become wealthy by selling lucrative restaurant franchises. Cherie was the smartest, kindest, strongest, funniest person he'd ever known. She was going to law school and wanted to help people.

That was where the rub started. He was driven, worked long hours, and only cared about getting ahead. She, on the other hand, thought she might end up a public defender or, better still, start a free legal office for the underprivileged in need of counsel.

"In the end, our differences drove us apart," Rhett admitted to Diane. "She was the one smart enough to pull the plug and declare our relationship over." It'd broken his heart, but he'd found solace in his work.

"So, that was it? The end of your romantic endeavors?"

"Well, I dated some—off and on. A few years back, I met a woman who worked at my firm. She was as driven as I was, which introduced its own set of difficulties. It's hard to build trust when you vie for the same top sales slots and the bonuses that brings. We drifted along for a couple of years until she met someone else—a guy she felt was better suited to her life goals." He let out a wry laugh. "And that's a quote. Frankly, while the end of those relationships smarted a bit, I knew neither of them was really right, you know?" His hand went to her hair. He ran his fingers lightly through her long blonde curls. "In some ways, it felt good to move on," he repeated. "This might sound overly sentimental, but I have watched my parents for years. I know what a good relationship looks like, and I want that."

Her face filled with conflict. Rhett could tell she desperately wanted to let her past go, to be brave and venture ahead. People weren't meant to be alone. He wasn't meant to be alone. "Diane, I can't promise much," he said, trying once again to reassure her. "But I vow never to hurt you."

Her face filled with longing. "I know—I do know that," she said with a light breath. She made the admission as if trying to convince herself of the truth of it. Then, she surprised him by leaning forward. "I want—" Her voice drifted, but her intention was clear from the look in her eyes.

Rhett felt a warm rush rise up inside him. She wanted him.

He slipped his hand around the back of Diane's neck, moved closer. Her lips parted.

Suddenly, his cell phone rang in his pocket.

"Blast it!" he growled. Angry, he pulled the dreaded thing out and glanced to see who had interrupted their moment.

The caller was unidentified, but he recognized the area code. It was a Chicago number. He reluctantly pulled the phone to his ear. "Yeah?"

"Rhett, I'm glad I caught you," the voice said through the phone. "This is Richard Manicke."

Rhett's heart lurched. What was the president of Chicago Private Equity Group calling him for?

Out of instinct, he stepped away a few feet for privacy. When the call ended, he returned to where Diane was sitting.

He held out the phone and stared at it, still not entirely believing the conversation he'd just had. "That was the top guy at my old firm," he told her.

"Yeah? What did he want?"

"They've fired my former boss, Judith Sandidge. They want me to return and take her place." While he felt sorry for Judith, he couldn't help but smile at the thought of her experiencing exactly what she'd dished out to him.

Before he could explain further, Diane visibly withdrew. She stood.

He reached for her, but she held up an open hand. "No, Rhett. You don't have to explain." She turned away from him and sprinted down the path.

Stunned at what had just transpired, he watched as she picked up the pace, turned and headed for the house.

23

Rhett raced after Diane as she sprinted across the lawn. Nearly out of breath, he caught up and grabbed her arm. "Diane? What's the matter? Why are you running?"

She turned to face him, her face mottled with frustrated tears. "Don't you see? I told you. I didn't want to fall for you. I can't do this—not to myself, to Stacey. Worse, I can't take the risk to my sobriety."

"Diane, what are you talking about?"

Her hands went to the sides of her face and she closed her eyes. "I can't."

"Can't?" Rhett reached for her, but she pulled away.

The back door opened and Grace appeared, followed by Ellen and Jared. "Everything all right?" Rhett's mom asked.

Diane drew a deep breath and quickly wiped at her face. "We're fine," she lied. To prove it, she lifted her lips in a wide smile.

Both mothers marched the short distance and joined them.

"Honey, what's the matter?" Ellen parked her hands on her hips, turned to Rhett. "Did you do something to her?"

"No," Rhett argued. "I didn't do anything." He paused, wondering why he felt the need to defend himself. "We were talking...about our relationship. I got a call."

Diane pushed a strand of sweaty hair off her forehead, now clearly embarrassed over her reaction. She took a deep breath. "I'm sorry," she said, keeping that faltering smile firmly in place. "Rhett didn't do anything. I—well, he's leaving. Rhett's going back."

His mother lifted her eyebrows. "What do you mean?" She turned to Rhett. "You're going back?"

"He intends to return to Chicago," Diane explained. She lifted her chin, trying to pull in her emotions and collect herself. "He's been offered a job back at his old firm." She reached for Rhett's arm. "Look, I'm happy for you. I know you've worked hard and deserve this."

Ellen and Grace glanced at each other, confused.

Jared ran his hand through the side of his hair. "Wait. You're leaving? What about Dad?" His expression turned dark. "And the oyster farm? You said you were in this for the long haul. What? Did that mean until something better came along?" Disgusted, he pivoted and heading for the house without waiting for his brother to respond.

"Wait!" Rhett called out. "Everyone, please. You owe it to me to let me explain." He looked at Diane. "All of you."

"Yes, I have a new job," he admitted. "But it's not back in Chicago."

He told them about the call from Richard Manicke, explaining that he'd been shelved at the equity firm for making the decision to remain here in Pacific Bay. "I made a decision to stay, at least for a while, so I could help sort things out with Pop, and all," Rhett explained. "And then we got Dr. Michaels's diagnosis. That changed everything."

He went on to report his call with Judith Sandidge, how she wasn't willing to let his personal needs come before those of the firm. She'd forced him off the Markowitz account which led to his resignation, especially when Rhett realized he was needed here permanently.

"Well, of all the—I've never heard of such a thing!" Grace said, not taking the news well. "I thought you simply resigned. I didn't know you were pushed out." She parked her hands on her hips and scowled. "You helped build that firm. I, for one, know you often worked round the clock to close deals. Did she even consider how much you contributed to the success of that place?"

His mother's indignation brought him a strange sense of comfort. She'd always been in his corner. No doubt, she remained his strongest supporter.

"Well, what goes around comes around, I guess. Apparently, in my absence, the Markowitz deal went down the drain. The board of directors laid the blame directly at Judith Sandidge's feet, so to speak. They voted unanimously to invite her out."

Grace couldn't help herself. Her face broke into a wide smile. "And they called you to take over."

Rhett nodded. "Yes, that they did." He looked over at Diane. "I admit, it felt good to be vindicated, at least in part. And the compensation package they are dangling is nothing to sneeze at."

Diane bit at her lip, listening intently without comment.

Rhett stepped closer to her, looked her directly in the eyes. "But I'm afraid I can't accept."

His mother was the first to ask why. Jared echoed her sentiment. "You mean, you're not going back?"

Rhett glanced across at their faces. He grinned. "Can't. Like I tried to explain, I already accepted a job in Portland."

Now, it was Ellen's turn to voice surprise. "Portland? What's in Portland?"

"The Brain Institute," Rhett explained. "Dr. Michaels contacted me a while ago. I didn't tell you earlier because we were still nailing down all the details, but I'm going to head up a new foundation they are establishing to fund research. Very expensive research." He turned back to Diane, placed his hand on her arm. "I will buy a place here in Pacific Bay and only be in Portland for necessary meetings. There will be occasions I'll have to travel beyond that, but only days at a time."

Jared looked skeptical. "But wait. I thought you were going to take over for Dad here at the oyster farm."

Rhett gripped his brother's shoulder. "Someone already has that job. Someone who is very capable and reliable. I'll be here to help, of course. Just like I always had been. Dad will contribute, too, until he no longer is able. But the day-to-day operation is yours, bro."

Rhett turned his attention back to Diane, who was clearly overwhelmed with relief. "As for this young lady, well—I intend to spend a lot of time with her." He placed his fingers under her chin and lifted her face to his. "And not as merely friends."

He pulled her close. "Just to be clear, I'm looking for something real. A relationship. You think you're ready for that?"

She ran her hands over his chest. "Yes," she responded. "I'd like that, too."

Rhett smiled in spite of himself. Months back, he'd thought he was coming to Pacific Bay for simply a visit. His pop's diagnosis had changed everything. Mostly, it changed him. He realized there was more to life than closing the next deal and climbing the corporate ladder. There was family. And the possibility of love with a woman he greatly admired.

His mom was right. Despite inevitable storms, life was good in between the rains. When you think you've been hijacked by circumstances, placed on hold—really, you're just making room for the magic moments. Moments that become the memories you'll cherish for the rest of your life.

Diane stared at him through a mist of tears.

Over the course of his adult life, Rhett had signed off on

more than his share of important transactions. He knew he wanted Diane. He was beginning to believe she wanted him back, but the ball was firmly in her court. There was no hurry. He had all the time in the world to close this deal. The first step would be to concentrate on making her happy. Starting right now.

Despite the fact everyone was watching, he leaned in closer and cradled Diane's jaw with his fingers, lifting her face to his. She caught her breath just before his lips found hers.

The taste of her mouth was heady and sweet. A soft moan escaped her lips.

He felt his own breath shallow, his gut tighten. His mouth descended again, dominant and possessive until her lips wholly surrendered to his.

"I—I'm glad you're staying," she finally whispered, tears streaming her cheeks.

The door to the house suddenly opened, and Wylie stepped onto the back deck, followed by Billy and little Levi.

"Hey," Wylie called out. "These kids tell me it's Thanksgiving. Doesn't that mean we should eat dinner pretty soon?"

Grace threw back her head and laughed. "Don't worry. We're coming, honey."

SNEAK PEAK

UNDER A MAUI SKY
The Maui Island Series - Book 1

Chapter 1

Ava Briscoe took a deep breath and leaned forward to check her appearance in the bamboo-framed mirror on the wall above the sink. "Goodness," she thought. "This dress and pearls make me look...well, old." Like most women living on the island of Maui, she'd much prefer wearing a comfortable, loose-fitted garment, something happy and bright-colored.

She pulled the tube of lipstick to her mouth, then leaned a little closer. It was true. A person's eyesight goes the minute you turn forty. In her case, forty had come and gone. She'd been wearing readers and misplacing them for years.

As Ava drew the color over her lips, she couldn't help but notice the dark circles under her eyes. No amount of that miracle product she'd ordered from Amazon had erased the tell-tale signs she hadn't slept in days.

"Mom?" Christel peeked her head through the bathroom door. "I think it's about time."

Ava smiled weakly back at her oldest daughter and pushed the lid back on her lipstick tube. "Okay."

"You alright, Mom?"

Ava forced a brightness in her voice. "Sure, honey. No need to worry." She moved to join her daughter at the door, smoothed her dress. "I just want to see your dad a minute first."

Christel slowly nodded. "Yeah, okay. Sure. Want me to go with—"

"No," Ava quickly assured her. "I'll join you in a minute."

Christel nodded a second time. "Okay. I love you, Mom."

"I love you too, baby." Ava turned and took one final glance in the mirror, pressed a stray curl back in place, then headed for the door.

The church foyer was now nearly empty as she walked across the tiled floor past the open double doors leading outside to the gardens. A slight breeze carried the scent of plumeria and white ginger and blew that stray curl out of place again. Ava gave up and tucked the rogue piece of hair behind her ear for good measure.

Wailea Seaside Chapel was located on Molokini Bluff with breathtaking ocean views and luxurious grounds. The chapel was like something out of a fairytale and featured soaring rafters, hand-carved wooden pews, and stained-glass windows. She and Lincoln had been married here, as had her younger daughter, Katie.

A ukulele played from inside the chapel where the others were gathered. She couldn't help herself. The corners of her lips turned up slightly as she recognized her favorite song —*Somewhere Over the Rainbow*. The version by Israel Kamakawiwo'ole, or Iz, as people on the island called him.

Her hand went to the knob on the closed door to the right

of the potted Bromeliad plant. She pushed the door ajar slightly, listened to make sure only her husband was in the room. Detecting no one, she entered.

"Lincoln, can you hear that? They're playing our song," she said, as she neared her husband. She reached and straightened his tie, then pulled the lapels of that awful suit into alignment. "Remember? That was the song that was playing that first night at the Grand Wailea."

Ava had been less than twenty years old when she met Lincoln Briscoe at her best friend's wedding. She was the maid of honor. Lincoln, the best man.

From the moment she laid eyes on him, her focus was scattered, so filled with nervous anticipation, even giddy. When they were seated next to each other at the luau reception, she couldn't even hold a conversation. Her thoughts danced in infinite directions as they lifted glasses in a toast to their friends, the newly married couple. She could picture the scene already —the two of them holding hands on their first date. He would take her for a long bare-footed walk on Mokapu Beach and watch the sun set behind craggy black rocks with towering palms.

Amazing thing? It had been just like that.

Of course, years of marriage had rubbed the shine off a bit. Raising four children and running a pineapple plantation could do that to a couple. Even so, their marriage had remained solid, reliable. They loved each other. For that, she was grateful.

"Well, honey. I guess it's time." An uninvited tear rolled down Ava's cheek. Fighting to breathe, she leaned and kissed her husband's forehead.

For the last time.

"Thank you, Lincoln," she whispered close to his ear. "You made me very happy. I—well, I loved you more than I can say." She choked back a sob and lifted. Now was not the time. There would be months, even years, ahead to miss this man—the man she'd loved.

She swept her hand across his chest, gave a final pat.

It was then she noticed a tiny corner from a piece of paper peeking out from the pocket of Lincoln's jacket. Ava scowled with curiosity and tugged the note free, opened it. Scrawled across the paper in handwriting were the words *Ua ola loko i ke aloha*.

She scowled.

Who in the world had placed the note in her husband's pocket? One of the children, maybe? And what did the words mean?

After living on Maui for as long as she had, Ava had assimilated into Hawaiian culture to some extent, yet her vocabulary still remained somewhat limited.

"Ava. Sweet hoaloha. Are you ready?"

She turned to see her closest friend peeking her head inside the door, her face filled with sympathy.

"It's time."

Ava mustered a weak nod. "Yes, Alani. I'm ready." Ava lifted her chin, bit at her trembling lip. She tucked the note inside her bag. With one final look back over her shoulder, she followed her friend out the door.

~ Chapter 2 ~

After the funeral service at the church, everyone gathered on the grounds of Pali Maui, the pineapple plantation she and Lincoln had owned and managed for nearly their entire married life.

Together, they had turned the fledgling operation she'd inherited into not only a profitable pineapple enterprise, but also a favorite tourist destination. They'd also raised their four children here. Ava could think of no better place in which to hold a final tribute to her husband.

Even so, she couldn't help but wish this day was over and she was free to crawl in bed. She was exhausted and tired of holding a smile on her face.

Katie appeared carrying a plate of what looked to be her luscious kalua pig with a generous helping of pineapple rice on the side. "Mom, you need to eat something," she urged, pressing the plate into Ava's hand.

"Oh, honey. I can't right now." Ava gave her a weak smile. "Maybe later."

Katie hesitated before she nodded. "Okay, but—"

Ava patted her daughter's arm. "I'm fine, honey. Please don't worry about me."

Funny, she should say that. Of course, they were worrying about her. She was worrying about them. She had ever since the night of that fateful call.

Ava rubbed her forehead against the ache forming. The road to Hana was known to be a dangerous drive, especially in a downpour. Why would Lincoln venture in that direction? Why hadn't he told her where he was going and the reason?

She caught the concern painted on Katie's face and forced a smile. She reached for the plate. "Look, I'll take this inside the house and put it in the refrigerator for later." She didn't tell her daughter that doing so would provide an excuse for a quick break from the crowd.

Lincoln knew hundreds of people and it seemed they were all here now, wanting to express their condolences, and share their memories. Ava slowed on her way to the house near a couple of men, picking up on their conversation.

"So many times, Lincoln was pushed to go the way of Dole and move the entire enterprise to Costa Rica." Miguel Nakamoa, their operations manager, let out an amused laugh. "And you know what Lincoln told them?"

The men leaned in to hear the remaining story, a tale they'd heard often out of Lincoln's own mouth.

"That's right," Mig nodded. "He told them to sit on their pokey pineapple crowns. He would never leave the island."

Ava smiled to herself as she continued walking. Actually, it had been her decision to remain on Maui. Her father would have wanted it that way. Lincoln had initially argued, reminding her that becoming a vertically integrated producer was the only way they would prosper and grow. Increasing labor costs on the island would slice away at their profit margin. Land was limited and distribution options were narrowing. Moving offered remedies to all these issues, and more. "That wouldn't mean *we* would move, Ava," Lincoln had argued. "We'd simply transfer the planting operation, harvesting and distribution aspects to Costa Rica."

Pali Maui was located south of the town of Wailuku and consisted of nearly fifteen hundred acres tucked against the western edge of Maui's lush Kahalawai mountains. They grew primarily pineapple, but also a few acres of banana, papaya, starfruit, coffee, guava, coconut, mango, and macadamia nuts. Tram buses toured the grounds. There was a retail operation that sold farm-fresh items grown on the farm, as well as apparel and souvenirs. The Restaurant at Pali Maui epitomized the farm-to-table concept—and then some. Presenting inventive dishes inspired by the plantation's crops, the beautiful open-air venue was frequently deemed one of the most romantic restaurants on the island.

She'd stood firm. "My dad bought this farm and entrusted it to me, believing we had a responsibility to give back to the people and culture who so graciously extended *e komo mai*. Our family was welcomed with open arms. The island of Maui is our home, Lincoln."

Inside the house, Ava found her granddaughter nestled against the sofa cushions, her attention buried in her phone.

She looked up. "Hey, Tutu."

The Hawaiian term warmed her heart. "Hey, Willa. What are you doing, sweet girl?"

She shrugged. "Just texting some friends."

Ava extended the plate in her direction. "Would you mind placing this in the refrigerator? I just—well, I need a minute."

Her granddaughter nodded and lifted from the couch. "Sure."

Ava gave her a grateful smile and wandered into her bedroom and shut the door, relishing the quiet. She'd barely had a moment to herself since hearing the news. She closed her eyes against the memory of that call, and then the officers at her door. Until that moment, she'd had no idea how quickly life could tumble upside down. How your foundation could be pulled from under your feet, leaving you in a free fall.

She wandered across the carpeted floor and folded into a chair next to a bookcase filled with volumes. They both loved to read, Lincoln especially.

He seemed to be everywhere. His voice, his presence. At times, even his smell.

Especially in this room.

Ava kicked off her shoes, leaned against the overstuffed back of the chair and closed her eyes for a brief rest.

She and Lincoln had married early, barely out of their twenties. It seemed like they had no more vowed their commitment to one another and she became pregnant.

Christel was their oldest. Her daughter was known to be a little high-strung, always had been. At two, she appeared at their bedroom door wearing a scowl. When asked what was wrong, Christel simply said, "Are you guys going to boss me today?"

The memory brought a smile to Ava's face. It was that same spunk that had propelled her girl onto the dean's list at Loyola. Much to Lincoln's dismay, their daughter had become very liberal, even dying her hair blonde in solidarity with her favorite candidate, Hilary Clinton. Lucky for them, she'd brought her legal talents back home from Chicago and joined the family business. She now managed all the legal and financial aspects of Pali Maui.

Katie was born four years later. Katie was—well, driven. While raising two girls of her own, she single-handedly expanded Pali Maui to include the tourist aspect of their family business, primarily the retail operation and restaurant. Lucky for them, she married one of the best chefs around. Katie was a brilliant marketer. The family could barely keep up with all her plans.

Then came the boys. Neither were married. Aiden was twenty-five and an EMT. Shane was two years younger and attended the University of Hawaii here on the island and had yet to decide his career path. If left up to him, he might never settle down. Lincoln often accused her of coddling their youngest son, but she knew Shane was simply a free spirit who loved his *pau hana*.

They'd raised an amazing family—a family that was now her sole responsibility. The burden felt heavy without Lincoln by her side to help shoulder the obligation of influencing, guiding and nurturing them emotionally. Parenting is the one job you never quit.

A future without Lincoln seemed a daunting thing. Yet, she knew this. She had to pick herself up and go on. She had to find a way to survive the loss and keep Pali Maui, its employees and her family on steady ground.

She would do it, she promised. Ava clenched her fists with determination.

So, help her. She would do it.

NOTE FROM THE AUTHOR:
I hope you've enjoyed this preview of UNDER A MAUI SKY

which is scheduled to release Spring 2021 and can be preordered now. Purchase links to all my books, including this one, can be found on my website:

www.kelliecoatesgilbert.com

ABOUT THE AUTHOR

Kellie Coates Gilbert has won readers' hearts with her compelling and highly emotional stories about women and the relationships that define their lives. A former legal investigator, Kellie's deep understanding of human nature is woven into every page.

In addition to garnering hundreds of five-star reviews, Kellie has been described by RT Book Reviews as a "deft, crisp storyteller." Her books were featured as Barnes & Noble Top Shelf Picks and were included on Library Journal's Best Book List of 2014.

Born and raised near Sun Valley, Idaho, Kellie now lives with her husband of over thirty-five years in Dallas, where she spends most days by her pool drinking sweet tea and writing the stories of her heart.

www.kelliecoatesgilbert.com

ALSO BY KELLIE COATES GILBERT

THE PACIFIC BAY SERIES

Chances Are

Remember Us

Chasing Wind

Between Rains

THE SUN VALLEY SERIES

Sisters

Heartbeats

Changes

Promises

LOVE ON VACATION SERIES

Otherwise Engaged

All Fore Love

TEXAS GOLD SERIES

A Woman of Fortune

Where Rivers Part

A Reason to Stay

What Matters Most

Made in the USA
Monee, IL
02 July 2021